CHILDREN OF
JUBILEE

CHILDREN OF EXILE:
BOOK 3

CHILDREN
OF
JUBILEE

MARGARET PETERSON
HADDIX

SIMON & SCHUSTER BOOKS FOR YOUNG READERS
NEW YORK   LONDON   TORONTO   SYDNEY   NEW DELHI

SIMON & SCHUSTER BOOKS FOR YOUNG READERS

An imprint of Simon & Schuster Children's Publishing Division

1230 Avenue of the Americas, New York, New York 10020

This book is a work of fiction. Any references to historical events, real people, or real places are used fictitiously. Other names, characters, places, and events are products of the author's imagination, and any resemblance to actual events or places or persons, living or dead, is entirely coincidental.

Text copyright © 2018 by Margaret Peterson Haddix

Cover photographs copyright © 2018 by Thinkstock

For information about special discounts for bulk purchases, please contact Simon & Schuster Special Sales at 1-866-506-1949 or business@simonandschuster.com.

The Simon & Schuster Speakers Bureau can bring authors to your live event.

For more information or to book an event, contact the Simon & Schuster Speakers Bureau at 1-866-248-3049 or visit our website at www.simonspeakers.com.

Also available in a Simon & Schuster Books for Young Readers hardcover edition

Book design by Greg Stadnyk

The text for this book was set in Weiss Std.

Manufactured in the United States of America

1019 OFF

First Simon & Schuster Books for Young Readers paperback edition December 2019

2 4 6 8 10 9 7 5 3 1

The Library of Congress has cataloged the hardcover edition as follows:

Names: Haddix, Margaret Peterson, author.

Title: Children of Jubilee / Margaret Peterson Haddix.

Description: First edition. | New York : Simon & Schuster Books for Young Readers, [2018] | Series: Children of exile ; 3 | Summary: Kiandra Watanaboneset reluctantly takes charge when she, her brothers Enu and Edwy, and some young friends are captured by Enforcers and sent to a prison on the planet Zacadi.

Identifiers: LCCN 2017025182 (print) | LCCN 2017039128 (eBook) | ISBN 9781442450110 (eBook) | ISBN 9781442450097 (hc) | ISBN 9781442450103 (pbk)

Subjects: | CYAC: Brothers and sisters—Fiction. | Adventure and adventurers—Fiction. | Extraterrestrial beings—Fiction. | Prisoners—Fiction. | Life on other planets—Fiction. | Science fiction.

Classification: LCC PZ7.H1164 (eBook) | LCC PZ7.H1164 Chd 2018 (print) | DDC [Fic]—dc23

LC record available at https://lccn.loc.gov/2017025182

For strangers who became friends

CHILDREN OF JUBILEE

CHAPTER ONE

"Run! Hide!" my brother Enu screamed beside me.

Enu had been trying to boss me around my whole life. Usually I resisted. But the sound I'd thought was thunder kept striking louder and louder behind us. It was the sound of marching feet.

Enforcers' marching feet.

Coming toward us.

I leaned forward, bent my knees, and shoved off the pavement, trying to launch myself through a gap in the crowd ahead.

This is not my life, I thought.

I was a tech geek. A coder. A hacker. A *Why leave the couch when everything's available online?* type. I never ran.

A hand grabbed my arm from behind.

"We have to stay together!" someone yelled.

Edwy. My *little* brother. The brother I'd never met until a few weeks ago. The one who'd always been kept safe.

Until . . . well, a few weeks ago.

"We need you!" he begged. Because I guess I was still barreling forward.

Oh, momentum . . . It's not just a scientific theory.

I whirled around. There must have been hundreds of people around us scrambling to escape. Maybe thousands. Maybe the entire population of Refuge City. But I got something like tunnel vision: My eyes could focus only on five faces. Three belonged to twelve-year-olds: Edwy and his friends Rosi and Zeba. Two belonged to five-year-olds: Rosi's little brother, Bobo, and a girl named Cana. Until a few weeks ago I'd never seen such young children in person, not since I was that age myself. When, of course, being that little seemed natural. But now it was hard to believe that such tiny human beings as five-year-olds were real. They seemed more like dolls or toys.

"Kiandra, will you carry me?" Cana asked, raising her arms to me. "I'm scared."

Me too, kid, I thought.

"Enu's the one with muscles," I said, backing away from her. Where was Enu?

He'd shoved his way farther into the crowd ahead of us than I had, but I grabbed for his hand and jerked him back. Because suddenly it hit me that Edwy was right: We did need to stick together. With the Enforcers invading Refuge City, we wouldn't be able to find one another electronically. How much longer would it be safe to use anything electronic at all?

Not . . . able . . . to . . . use . . . electronics. . . .

It was a horrifying thought. I glanced down at the stolen Enforcer communication device in my hand. We'd taken it from one of the Enforcers we'd battled out in the desert. I was *mostly* confident that I'd managed to disable any tracking built into the device, just as I was *mostly* confident that I'd blocked all the bioscans for the entire city, so the seven of us kids wouldn't instantly be picked up as criminals.

Now would be a really bad time to be wrong.

"I want *you* to carry me, Kiandra," Cana insisted, grabbing my waist.

Now, what was that about? Granted, Bobo had already hopped up into Rosi's arms, so she wasn't available. But Cana had known Edwy her entire life—why wasn't he her first choice? Or Zeba, who liked taking care of people? Or Enu, who really did have a lot of muscles and could have carried Cana on his back without even noticing?

Cana wasn't the only one staring at me with wide, terrified eyes. Rosi, Zeba, Edwy, and now even Enu were too. And Bobo probably would have, except that he'd just buried his face against his sister's neck, letting her stare for both of them.

Oh. Everybody thinks I have a plan. Everyone thinks I can save them.

I tucked the Enforcer communication device under my arm and pulled out my mobile phone.

3

"We need to find the best hiding place," I told Enu. "*Before* we start running."

Someone or something—Enu? Zeba? Just the natural pressure of the screaming, fleeing crowd?—pushed us to the side, against the wall of a Ref City skyscraper. But I was lost in an electronic world, searching for maps of all the nearby basements. Type, type, swipe, maximize, minimize. . . . Just in case someone could track my search, I clicked on a building four blocks to the east, even as I announced to the group, "Follow me. We're going west."

Cana grabbed my shoulders and scrambled up onto my back—okay, whatever. I pulled the Enforcer communication device from beneath my arm and handed it to her.

"Hide this between us," I told her, and she obediently tucked it under her chin, against my back.

But then I felt bad, like I was endangering her too much. She was *five.*

I was so not used to watching out for anyone but myself.

We reached a deserted alleyway full of Dumpsters.

"The door at the end!" I shouted, pointing. "I hacked in and changed the security code for the keypad to eight-zero-nine-two. Go!"

I twisted around to pull Cana from my back and hand her to Enu. She held on tighter.

"Aren't you coming with us?" Cana asked.

No, not just Cana—Enu practically whimpered the same thing. Maybe the others did too. My ears had starting ringing so badly I could barely hear anything.

I broke Cana's hold on me and thrust her at Enu.

"After I hide this!" I yanked the Enforcer communication device from between Cana and me as it fell. "We don't want to be caught with it!"

Enu grabbed my wrist.

"We get caught, we're doomed anyway," he said. "We can't lose you."

This was the worst thing ever. Not the doomed part—I already knew that. It was Enu being sentimental and needy that slayed me. He'd spent the past thirteen years—my entire life—pretty much saying, "Why do I have to have a little sister? Sisters are useless! Why couldn't you have been the banished one? Why couldn't I have a brother instead?"

And then, just a matter of weeks ago, Edwy had shown up at our door.

Now look where we were: homeless fugitives, desperately fleeing the alien Enforcers.

And the Enforcers claimed they had the right to take over Ref City just because of something *we'd* done.

I wanted to make a joke about all this, to wisecrack, *Who's useless now?* I wanted all this to *be* a joke. Enu and me, we didn't do serious.

But this day was nothing but serious.

"I'm not going far," I said, my voice gruff. "I'll just hide it . . . over there."

I gestured at one of the Dumpsters. Strategically, this was really dumb. If the Dumpster was ever emptied again—if Ref City ever became that normal again—the communication device would be taken away. And it was insanity to keep the device in the same alleyway where we were hiding. How hard could it be to stash the device in the next alley over? Or—even better—a block or two away?

But I gazed out of the alley at the hordes flooding past on the street. Just in the few seconds since we'd ducked past the Dumpsters, the crowd had gone from panicked to frenzied to rabid. People were knocking one another down. People were trampling other people's bodies.

"Bobo and Cana can't see this," Rosi said. Her brother still had his face burrowed against her neck, but she put her hand on Cana's head, gently steering the younger girl to look toward the door leading to safety. "Come on."

She tugged Enu and Cana toward the door. Once Enu started moving, Rosi pulled Edwy and Zeba after them.

Zeba peered at me, her eyes wide with shock and horror.

"Kiandra, please—" she began.

"I'll be right behind you," I promised. I wanted to add, *Believe me, I'm no martyr. I know how to look out for number one.*

But that wasn't actually something I could promise. Not today.

I crouched low to hide in the shadow of the Dumpsters, and dashed to the nearest one. Then I slid the Enforcer communication device into the gap between the bottom of the Dumpster and the ground. Nobody would see it there.

Unless some rat comes along and noses it out into the open, I thought. *Unless . . .*

"Kiandra!"

Enu stood in the doorway at the end of the alley. I could see the others behind him, descending the stairs into darkness.

Should have stopped to grab flashlights, I thought. *Should have studied survival tips for life on the streets.*

I really hated situations I wasn't prepared for. Situations I couldn't study and analyze ahead of time.

But maybe my feet were smarter than my brain, because I started sprinting toward Enu and the doorway. When I was still a meter or two away, he reached out and pulled me in. The metal door began swinging shut behind us.

"Wait," I said, when there was only a narrow crack left between the door and the frame.

"Did you hear something? Is someone there?" Enu hissed at me. He was already three steps down the stairs. The others were far below. "Shut the door! Lock it!"

I hadn't heard anything new. I'd *stopped* hearing

something. The screams of the crowd, which had seemed endless just a moment ago, had suddenly ceased.

It was like air vanishing, like going deaf—something I'd taken for granted was suddenly gone.

I peeked out the crack beside the door, and after a second Enu joined me, standing on tiptoes to lean his chin against the top of my head.

The crowd fleeing ahead of the Enforcers had disappeared. But the thudding of the Enforcers' marching *hadn't* stopped. It had grown from a distant rumble to a constant roar, like thunderclaps so close together that the echo of one met the next striking crash.

Then the first line of Enforcers came into view out in the street: one black uniform after another, one long row after another of bubbled space helmets gleaming in the sunlight like a taunt: *You pitiful humans don't know how to fight us now. Not anymore. We've made ourselves indestructible, can't you see?*

Enu grabbed my shoulders and began to pull me away.

"They'll see us!"

"No, they won't!" I shoved him away. "Only if they use the bioscans, and if those work . . ."

If those work, there's nothing we can do, nowhere we can go. No way to save ourselves.

I didn't say that out loud.

"I just want to see what they do," I whispered. "I have to know . . ."

To know if we're doomed.

Enu put his hands on my shoulders again, but only to get closer to the door. He and I both pressed our faces against the crack and kept peeking out.

One of the Enforcers at the end of the row turned toward the alley, and my heart seized. He lifted a gun to his shoulder.

I clutched Enu's hand. There wasn't time to run. I could only watch.

But the Enforcer wasn't aiming at us. He pointed his gun at the Dumpster where I'd hidden the communication device. He squeezed his trigger.

Instantly the Dumpster vanished.

CHAPTER TWO

"Vaporized," Enu whispered numbly. "He just va—"

"Shh," I said.

The Enforcer stepped out of line. Almost casually, he began moving toward the spot where the Dumpster had been only a moment before—and toward us. But after only five or six steps he bent down and reached for something on the ground, something alongside the broken bottles and scorched weeds.

He picked up the communication device I'd hidden there.

"Does he know we're here?" Enu asked.

"Or does he think we were in the Dumpster?" I whispered back. "Was he trying to vaporize *us*?"

Or maybe I just moved my lips and no sound came out. Maybe those words were too terrifying to say aloud.

The Enforcer pocketed the communication device and turned back toward the rest of his squad. Did he glance our way first? His shadowy bubble helmet made it impossible to see.

"Kiandra? Enu? What are you doing? Aren't you coming with us?"

It was Edwy, calling up from the bottom of the stairway. Enu and I both reached for the door handle, but my hand was a little closer. I pulled the door all the way shut, waiting to hear the lock click into place before I turned. Enu's eyes met mine as he also spun around. And even though we had only a few weeks of experience with having a younger brother—and less than twenty-four hours of knowing the other four kids—it was like Enu and I were in instant agreement: *We can't tell Edwy or the others what we saw. It will scare them too much.*

"Just double-checking the lock, pipsqueak," Enu said. His voice cracked, split with fear. He might as well have screamed, *I just saw the most horrifying thing of my life! And it wasn't a video game, wasn't a movie, wasn't special effects— it really happened.*

Edwy just nodded.

"It's like a maze down here," he said. "Kiandra, do you have any idea which way we should go?"

My feet found the first step down. My brain liked that. It was screaming, *Get away from the Enforcers and their vaporizers! Go! Go! Go!* But all I said aloud was, "We're under the biggest grocery store in Ref City. Let's aim for their storeroom. We'll need food."

"Oh, yeah. Food," Enu echoed blankly, as if he barely even knew what that was.

Enu was fifteen. I'd seen him eat two large pizzas and twenty buffalo wings, then stand up and announce, "Okay, now I'm hungry again. Did you order anything else, or are you trying to starve me?"

He *never* forgot about food.

"So do you know where the storeroom is?" Edwy asked, as if I was the one being slow and stupid.

Automatically I reached for my phone.

"Are you sure you want to do that?" Enu whispered beside me.

I did. I didn't. What I *really* wanted was to go back to yesterday, when I didn't know much of anything about Enforcers. I wanted to be back then, and back in our penthouse apartment on the other side of Ref City, where the biggest thing I'd ever had to worry about was faking Enu's grades on the school website. That and figuring out how far it was safe to push Udans, the man who was our only link to our parents, and . . .

Oh, Udans.

My heart threatened to split wide open. Maybe it *did* break apart. The last time we'd seen him, Udans was driving a truck with six unconscious Enforcers hidden in the back. He was driving it *away* from all of us kids, because he wanted us to be safe.

If the Enforcers could track down the one solitary

disarmed communication device I'd carried off, they could certainly track down Udans and the missing Enforcers.

And if they vaporized a mere Dumpster, then . . .

I stumbled on the stairs, and Enu grabbed my arm to keep me from falling.

"I don't think my phone will work this far underground— and I should probably keep the battery for urgent uses. But if I remember the building layout right, you should turn to the left," I told Edwy.

"Okay," Edwy said.

Just a matter of hours ago, Edwy had been alone and surrounded by Enforcers. And *he'd* figured out what to do, how to outsmart the Enforcers, how to get Udans to help. If a twelve-year-old could outsmart the Enforcers, couldn't the brilliant leaders of Refuge City figure out a way to convince the Enforcers to leave?

Of course they can, I told myself. *So, really, all we have to do is hang out in the Emporium of Food storeroom eating like kings for a day or two, and then everything will go back to normal. The Enforcers will leave. And Ref City will go back to being its usual glitzy, beautiful, safe, sterile place. Where nothing I do actually matters.*

I didn't usually lie to myself. But it felt like I had to now, just to keep my feet moving.

Enu and I got to the bottom of the stairs, and we followed

the younger kids through a narrow, dirty hallway lit only by bare, fly-specked bulbs. The soles of my sandals kept sticking to the dark floor, and I tried not to think about what filth might be down there. Spilled milk? Squashed bits of rotten fruit?

Blood?

Rosi and Zeba both seemed to be tiptoeing. Rosi swayed under Bobo's weight. Earlier today *she'd* been running through the desert, desperately trying to escape from the Enforcers and get Cana and Bobo to safety.

"Bobo, you're a big boy," I said. "Why don't you get down and walk on your own?"

I tried to sound kind and cajoling like Mrs. Koseet, the nicest nanny Enu and I had ever had. But somehow my voice came out harsh and angry like, well, pretty much every other nanny Enu and I had ever had.

Even in the dim light I could see Bobo tighten his grip around his sister's shoulders, bunching together the fabric of her dirty, torn dress.

"He's okay," Rosi said wearily.

I felt Cana slide her hand into mine, and I didn't shake it away.

"Somebody needs to turn on a brighter light," Bobo complained. "Or we need windows. I can't *see*."

"Kiddo, we're in a basement," Enu said. His voice was as harsh as mine. "Basements don't have windows."

"Every basement did, that he's ever seen," Edwy said, like he was apologizing for Bobo. "Even if it was just those small, high-up windows you couldn't actually see through, made of blocks of glass . . ."

"Oh, we had those in my Fredtown too!" Zeba exclaimed.

Were we all in shock? Was that why they were talking about basements and windows, instead of the fact that we were probably all going to die very soon?

"Fredtowns," Enu growled, as if the word itself offended him.

It offended me, too. All the younger children—indeed, every kid on planet Earth who was twelve or younger—had been kidnapped at birth and raised until just a few weeks ago in safe, perfect little communities somewhere else in the universe. By safe, kind, supposedly perfect aliens called Freds. Nobody on Earth knew exactly where the Freds took the little kids, because, duh, of course humans would have united and attacked and brought them back.

Instead Earth's leaders had had to bargain and cajole and convince the intergalactic court that Earth wasn't such a bad place after all, and that it was safe for all the kids to come home.

That process had taken twelve years.

Meanwhile Enu and I—and all the other kids who were born even just a little bit more than twelve years ago—were shunted around and ignored and pretty much left to grow up on our own. Because Earth's parents could think of nothing but their lost children.

At least, that was how it had felt to *me*.

"It's not our fault where we grew up," Edwy said quietly. "None of us had a choice."

"We have a choice now," Enu grumbled, pointing to a split in the hallway ahead. "Which way, Kiandra?"

I automatically reached for my phone again—then drew my hand back. It wasn't worth the risk.

"Maybe . . . left again?" I said, my voice trembling. I hated not being sure. I hated the way my mind went fuzzy, trying to remember the blueprint of this basement.

I hated not being able to hold a phone or a tablet or a laptop in my hand and instantly *know* everything I wanted to know.

"It's okay if you're wrong," Zeba said comfortingly. "We know you're doing the best you can."

Why did that make me want to punch her in the face?

It was a good thing Cana had such a tight grip on my hand, or I might have.

All the younger kids obediently turned to the left. Enu narrowed his eyes menacingly at me but did the same.

The new hallway was even dimmer and dirtier than the first. But ahead of me Rosi, Zeba, and Edwy all stepped confidently, as if they totally trusted me. I studied the straight, perfect part in Zeba's hair, the strands on each side smoothed down into sleek braids. I watched Rosi grab Edwy's arm when he started to slip on an oily patch on the floor. Once he was steady again, she patted him encouragingly on the back.

Had I ever been that un-self-conscious?

Probably not. Even when I was four or five—Cana's age—I could remember worrying that if my hand brushed a boy's arm in our kindergarten class, that boy would think I liked him, the other girls would tease me, the teacher would tell me I needed to keep my hands to myself. . . .

What would I be like if I had grown up in a Fredtown? I wondered, not for the first time.

It didn't really matter. Either way, I'd be back on Earth now, and in danger from the Enforcers.

"Kiandra was right!" Cana suddenly crowed beside me. She pointed to a door to the side, one we'd almost walked past. Someone had scrawled a label on the door: STOREROOM.

"That kid knows how to read?" Enu muttered. "Isn't she only five?"

In our normal life, that would have been the cue for me to mock him: *I can see why you're amazed, since you barely know how to read* now. But being right made me feel so good, I kicked back into take-charge mode.

"Okay, here's what we do," I announced. "I'll pick the lock, and then—"

"Pick the lock?" Cana repeated. "You mean the door is locked, but you're going to make it open anyway? That doesn't sound like a good thing to do! When people put locks on things, you have to respect the other people's belongings."

"But people are more important than things, and the people who own this room would want us to be safe," Zeba explained gently. "And Kiandra thinks we need to go into this room to do that."

"Oh," Cana said.

I bit my tongue to keep from saying, *The people who own this room wouldn't care.* I gave Enu a little kick so he wouldn't say anything either. Then I balanced on one foot and pulled off the other sandal. I used the pointed part of the sandal's buckle to poke into the lock on the door. Was the tongue of the buckle long enough?

Click—success.

I turned the doorknob.

"Now, where did you learn *that*?" Edwy asked, his eyes wide and glowing.

I couldn't say, *Breaking into Enu's room when he wasn't around, what else?* with Enu standing right there. So I just bragged, "Stick with me. You'll learn all sorts of things."

My swagger melted away as soon as I put my sandal back on and we all shoved our way into the storeroom. This room was clean and bright—too bright. It was full of gleaming chrome counters that reflected our shocked, dirty faces.

Racks along the side overflowed with glistening strawberries, lettuce, grapes, radishes . . .

Any place that sterile and well lit had to be cleaned regularly. Produce that fresh had to be switched in and out at least once a day. Maybe even hourly.

"Quick," I said. "Grab as much food as you can carry, and let's get out of here."

Bobo poked his head up, so only his dark eyes showed over Rosi's shoulder.

"That would be *stealing*," he said. "Stealing is bad."

It was on the tip of my tongue to snarl back, *You don't even have green eyes, so what do you know?*

Good grief, where had *that* come from?

I knew—it was the kind of thing my parents believed. So did many others back in my miserable birthplace, Cursed Town. Plenty of people in Ref City thought that way too.

But *I* didn't. I wasn't like that.

Rosi patted Bobo's hair.

"Don't worry, little brother," she said. "We'll pay for everything we take. Then it's not stealing."

Zeba and Edwy reached for their pockets. Distress flowed over both their faces.

"When I put on these clothes, I thought I was just going to play a basketball game," Zeba muttered, tugging on her T-shirt and patting her netted shorts. "I don't have anything to pay *with*."

Enu started to pull up a pocket of his basketball shorts; then he shoved it down again.

"We can't leave a debit card behind," he said. "Not with my name on it. We can't let anyone know we were here. We can't leave a trail. . . ."

"Then we'll leave a note promising that we'll come back and pay," Rosi said in a firm voice.

"Except there's no paper," Edwy said, looking around. "Or anything to write with."

Seriously? We were running away from Enforcers who probably wanted to kill us, and these kids were going to stop and debate how to make it right to steal a radish?

Bobo started to cry.

"I'm *so* hungry," he said.

"We ran out of food, out in the desert," Rosi said, as if to apologize for her brother's whining and tears. "Bobo and Cana and I, we haven't eaten since . . . since . . ."

The corners of her mouth trembled, like she was about to cry, too.

"So—eat! Here!" I grabbed a handful of strawberries and held them out to her.

Rosi jerked back, as if I were trying to force-feed her poison.

"I can't set a bad example for Bobo," she mumbled.

Cana tugged on my arm.

"What if we eat the food, and then stay here until the nice store owner comes?" she asked, gazing up at me, her green eyes wide and innocent. "We can hide until we're sure it *is* the nice store owner, not someone who . . . who might want to hurt us. And we'll tell the nice store owner what happened, and he'll understand. And we'll make sure he gets his money. So everybody's happy."

"That's a good plan!" Zeba exclaimed.

Oh, right, I wanted to snarl. *Except for about ten billion reasons it isn't. Starting with—let's just go with the basic—when are store owners ever nice? Did you kids even grow up on Planet Earth?*

No, they hadn't. I didn't know why I couldn't keep that in my brain.

It was just . . . the younger kids *looked* so much like normal human beings. Edwy might as well have been Enu's clone from three years ago.

I gazed toward Enu, because I knew he wouldn't put up with this nonsense. But he shrugged.

"Okay," he said. "Whatever."

Bobo squealed and scrambled down. And then he grabbed a giant strawberry out of my hand and plopped the whole thing into his mouth.

"There's meat and cheese in the giant refrigerator over here," Edwy exclaimed, opening one stainless steel door after another. "And . . . ice cream in the freezer!"

As the younger kids ran around collecting food, I grabbed Enu's arm.

"You're faking them out, right?" I said. "After our stomachs are full, then we have to find a safer hiding place. We can't stay where everything's so bright. And where other desperate fugitives might figure out to come for food . . ."

Enu stopped in the middle of cramming grapes in his mouth. He leaned close, so only I would hear.

"Why are you acting like any of this matters?" he asked. He bit down hard on a grape. Some of the juice hit my cheek. "You can do whatever you want. I just decided I don't want to die on an empty stomach."

In my mind's eye, I saw the Enforcer vaporizing the Dumpster again—the Dumpster solid and heavy and *there* one moment, then zapped into nothingness the next. I could tell: That moment was scrolling again and again through Enu's brain too.

Enu thought we were going to meet the same fate as that Dumpster, no matter what we did. He *already* thought of us as nothing.

Enu had given up. And he thought I should too.

But I wasn't Enu.

CHAPTER THREE

Bobo was still chewing when he fell asleep.

"I'll just tuck him in over . . . uh, over there?" Rosi murmured, peering around.

She must have been looking for someplace safe and dark and hidden. But even the corners of the storeroom were brightly lit.

"We can take turns standing guard," Edwy said, wiping mustard off his face. "You can sleep first."

Was this really *my* brother being so sweet and noble? Edwy looked like such a mini-Enu, it threw me off whenever Edwy did something that wouldn't have even occurred to Enu.

How would Enu have turned out if he'd *been raised in a Fredtown?* I wondered.

My throat ached as I watched Rosi wrap a towel around Bobo like a blanket. Or, no—she was hiding him. She wasn't as stupid as I thought. Rosi, Zeba, and Cana curled up alongside the little boy, and Rosi began pulling towels over to hide Zeba's orange T-shirt and basketball shorts and Cana's green-and-brown dress as well.

"Enu," I whispered.

Enu kept mindlessly cramming sandwich halves into his mouth.

"I can't . . . ," I began. "I can't stay here."

Enu's eyes widened; even his dim-bulb brain had picked up on how I'd shifted from *we* to *I*.

Automatically my hand reached for the phone in my pocket. Then, resolutely, I let my hand drop. How many times had I repeated this process since the other kids had started eating? Fifty? A hundred?

"I mean, I can't just stay here without knowing how much danger we're in," I said. "How likely it is that we're going to be found. I have to know what's going on . . . outside."

Enu's eyes tracked the movement of my hand: reaching for the phone once again, then resolutely stopping.

"You're addicted to the Internet," he said. "It's like a drug that's going to kill you. And the rest of us too."

So now *he* was accusing *me* of giving up?

Food always had made Enu cocky.

"I'm *not* going to check anything on my phone," I said. "That's too dangerous. But those stairs over there have to lead up into the store. There'd be TVs, I bet. Maybe even a computer I could hack into on some office desk. A computer that *wouldn't* be linked to me, so no one would know I was the one using it. . . ."

"Sounds like too much of a risk to me," Enu complained through a mouthful of mushed-up bread and deli meat. "But . . . you're going to drive yourself crazy if you *don't* go up those stairs, right?"

I guess Enu knew me as well as I knew him.

Enu swallowed hard, probably gulping down an entire sandwich practically unchewed.

"I'm going with you," he said. "It's not like you could protect yourself on your own."

Why did he always have to turn something sweet and kind into a put-down?

"Edwy, get over here," he said, motioning with his head. Edwy obediently left the other kids behind.

"You two want to sleep too, while I'm standing guard?" Edwy asked eagerly, as if he could single-handedly fend off Enforcers.

Well, he did do pretty well on his own out in the desert, while Enu was hiding in a cave and I was locked in the truck. . . .

He'd also had Udans's help, back in the desert.

I couldn't let myself think about Udans.

Enu puffed out his chest, like he always did when he was showing off for Edwy. Just think how obnoxious Enu would be if he'd had a little brother idolizing him for the past twelve years, instead of just the past two weeks.

"Kiandra and I are going to scout around a little, get the lay of the land," he said. "You're in charge while we're away."

Right, because in Enu's opinion, any room Enu was in belonged to Enu. So of course when Enu left, Enu got to choose the next leader.

"Can't I go too?" Edwy asked.

Edwy was just a year younger than me. But the difference between twelve and thirteen was *huge*. Edwy still had rounded cheeks, almost like Bobo's. His arms reminded me of twigs or maybe pipe cleaners—not the boulders that Enu's biceps called to mind.

But out in the desert, I'd seen Edwy bravely walk *toward* the Enforcers chasing Rosi, even though he seemed to have no chance of rescuing her. It had done something to my heart. Before I'd known it, I was acting insanely brave too.

I couldn't stand to see Edwy rushing toward danger again.

"Didn't you just promise to stand guard for the others?" I asked.

"Oh, yeah," Edwy said, his face flushing. He bit his lip, then blurted, "Do you really think it's a good idea for us to split up?"

"Sure," Enu said, sounding as carefree as ever. "We'll be back before you know it."

Edwy didn't look like he believed Enu, which made me feel even more like I had to get away. Fast.

"Out of our way, squirt," I growled, scurrying for the stairs.

So when I get to the top of the stairs and some trigger-happy Enforcer instantly vaporizes Enu and me, those are the last words Edwy's going to remember me saying to him? I thought. *I'm as bad as Enu.*

I couldn't think about that right now. I couldn't think about trigger-happy Enforcers, either, or else I would freeze completely.

Enu and I reached the door at the top of the stairs, and I had to use my sandal buckle again to pick another lock.

"No sudden moves," I whispered to Enu. "We don't step out into the open anywhere, until we're sure it's safe."

Enu made a sound that might have been a skeptical snort, because none of this was safe. We hadn't been safe since we'd forced Udans to take us out into the desert.

No, really, we hadn't been safe since Edwy and the other younger children had come back from their Fredtowns.

Maybe we hadn't been safe since we were born. Maybe safety had always been an illusion.

I opened the door a crack. I saw dark shadows, but they were only empty tables and empty chairs. Good. We weren't facing into the store itself, just some employee workroom that was deserted.

"Coast is clear," I murmured to Enu.

Both of us slipped into the dark room, leaving the door ajar behind us. The only light came from beside the door, where a giant screen displayed staticky lines and fuzz.

"There's a TV, but it's broken," Enu said, the disappointment heavy in his voice.

"Or the Enforcers stopped all the broadcasts," I muttered.

"Could they . . . could they shut down the Internet, too?" Enu asked.

"Sure," I said, as though this didn't make my stomach churn and my palms sweat.

Maybe Enu was right. Maybe I was addicted to the Internet.

I skirted past the flickering TV screen and tiptoed toward the door at the opposite side of the room. I had my hand on the doorknob when a voice suddenly boomed behind me: "Attention, Refuge City!"

CHAPTER FOUR

It was just the TV.

But who's controlling it?

Enu was reaching out to punch my arm. He was probably about to say something stupid like, *Hey, look! The TV isn't broken, after all! Do you see? Do you see it's working now?*

But I was already reacting. I whipped around and tackled him.

Normally, Enu could have flicked me away like an annoying bug. He outweighed me by at least twenty-five kilograms of solid muscle. But I had the element of surprise on my side. I knocked him to the floor.

"What are you doing?" Enu protested, but I already had my hand over his mouth.

"Sometimes," I whispered in his ear, "TVs work like spy cameras. While we're watching them, they could be watching *us*."

Enu nodded, and I slid my hand off his face. We rolled

over behind one of the chairs, and I lifted my head just enough to peek at the TV from across the tabletop. Enu crept up beside me.

Normally, sitting beside Enu was like hanging out with a water buffalo. He took up all the room. Sometimes I swore he breathed in all the air, and there was none left for me. But right now it felt like Enu had shrunk. I leaned my shoulder against his just to make sure he was still there.

A familiar face appeared on the TV screen: a TV anchorman named Daniel Brockteau. His smile was as self-assured as ever, his dark hair as slicked-back and perfect as always.

"We are reporting live on the arrival of our rescuers in Refuge City," he says. "The Enforcers have generously consented to stay as long as needed to ensure peace and prosperity."

I thrust my hand out to cover Enu's mouth again, because it would be just like him to yell, *They're aliens, not rescuers! They're not even human! They're not being generous—they're evil! People were running away in terror!*

But maybe I'd overestimated Enu's processing speed. He just sat there with his jaw dropped, like he didn't understand.

And, really . . . I'm the one more likely to yell at a TV screen.

"We have a special guest here in the news studio," Daniel

Brockteau announced, smoothly gathering up papers on the desk before him. "Sir?"

The camera scanned to the right, where a second man sat at the adjoining desk.

No, not a man, I thought. *An Enforcer.*

The bubblelike space helmet around his head was a dead giveaway, but I think I would have known anyway. The Enforcer's eyes were too cold and beady; the human face he wore under the helmet looked a little too fake.

But doesn't Daniel Brockteau's face look fake too? I tested myself. *Like he's had plastic surgery, like every pore of his skin is covered with makeup?*

It wasn't the same. I couldn't explain it, even to myself, but I still looked at Daniel Brockteau and instantly categorized him as human, and looked at the Enforcer and instantly thought, *Not.*

And yet Edwy had told me that the entire time he'd lived in Fredtown—all his life until the past few weeks—he'd never realized that the Freds were aliens too. He'd never known that he *wasn't* on Earth.

So Freds and Enforcers are both aliens, but they're not the same kind of aliens. Freds are better at passing as humans.

Or Edwy had just been incredibly naïve. Like everyone else raised in a Fredtown.

"Allow me to introduce myself," the Enforcer said. "I am

General DeMonde, supreme commander of Enforcer operations on Earth. I thank all of you for inviting us to your lovely planet."

Enu's jaw dropped farther. I clenched my teeth together as hard as I could, and still a gurgle sounded in my throat, the only remnant of the words I wanted to scream: *We didn't invite you here! You invaded!*

Enu put his hand on my arm, and I shook it away.

"We also appreciate how cooperative we've found the native populace," General DeMonde continued. "We are now in charge and in control of every part of Planet Earth. And I am pleased to report that the transfer of power has been entirely peaceful and without incident."

I thought about the Dumpster vanishing before my eyes. I thought about how the crowd running from the Enforcers had been screaming, and then . . . they weren't. And they weren't anywhere in sight.

I thought about how many things I wasn't letting myself think.

"He's lying!" I hissed at Enu. "We're not going to find out anything watching TV!"

But Enu wasn't listening. Enu was springing to his feet. Enu was grabbing a chair.

Enu hurled the chair at the TV screen, and it shattered in a spray of broken glass.

CHAPTER FIVE

"That wasn't very smart," I whispered into the silence after the glass stopped falling.

"You don't understand," Enu said. He was breathing hard. Enu bragged about being able to play three basketball games in a row without breaking a sweat; I knew he wasn't worn out just from throwing a chair. "I *had* to do that."

I sighed.

"I do understand," I whispered back. "But . . . we can't stay here now."

Enu looked at the door that led back to the basement, then to the door across from it, the one I'd been about to open when the TV came on. The one that led into the unknown.

"Which way?" he asked.

"If someone comes, we need to lead them away . . . away from the other kids." Suddenly I had a huge lump in my throat. "We have to go *now*."

I made myself stand up and reach for the knob of the

mystery door again. It turned easily, but a long moment passed before I could work up the courage to actually pull the door open.

For the other kids, I told myself. *You have to.*

The door swung back, and . . .

More darkness. But no one leaped out at us. No row of Enforcers stood there, ready to shoot. Instead I saw hulking shapes taller than my head, bathed in shadow.

Shelves, I told myself. *They're just shelves.*

Enu and I were facing the emporium part of the Emporium of Food. The store. And it was after hours, so the emporium was closed and empty. Or, no—it never closed. Enu and I had placed orders at three a.m. before, and then a delivery person always showed up at our door ten or fifteen minutes later.

The store was closed and silent tonight because of the invasion.

Just then I heard a crash coming from the opposite side of the store. Or maybe it was even outside, in the street.

"Would the Enforcers break in to come and get us?" Enu asked, clutching my shoulder.

Or would they just vaporize the entire building? I wondered.

A second crash sounded, and then a thud. I put the sounds together: Enu wasn't the only one throwing heavy things at glass tonight.

"Rocks," I whispered to Enu. "Through the windows. Doesn't seem like an Enforcer strategy."

"So it's people doing that?" Enu asked, craning his neck as if he had some hope of seeing over the tall row of shelves before us. "Other human beings?"

Refuge City had always been one of the safest places on Earth—it had been designed that way from the very beginning. But unlike Enu, I'd watched my history lessons; I'd seen what had happened in other parts of the world, at other times. I could call up images in my mind of people rebelling, rioting, looting. Bricks or rocks thrown through a window were always followed by hordes of people streaming into a store, ripping items off shelves, maybe even starting fires that burned down entire buildings and trapped people inside. . . .

I strained my ears, listening. I could hear nothing else from the other side of the store.

No, I could hear one thing: a scraping sound. Was it actually a cricket? No one *ever* heard crickets in Refuge City, because of all the traffic and the honking horns and the music from street performers and just the crowds of people talking and talking and talking. . . .

"We have to go see what's happening," I told Enu.

He nodded. I was glad his face was entirely in shadow, because otherwise I might have seen how scared he was. This way I could lie to myself; I could tell myself *he* wasn't afraid, and that no matter what, my big, brave brother would protect me.

I took the first step. Staying in the deepest shadows, we tiptoed down an aisle to the center of the store, then skulked from one hiding place to another, one shelf to the next. Finally we reached the last row of shelves before the outside window.

"We're not going all the way out there, are we?" Enu whispered in my ear, and even speaking so softly his voice squeaked. He seemed as young as Edwy suddenly.

He wasn't going to protect me. He couldn't. He was more likely to do something foolish and rash that put us both in more danger.

Something *else*, I mean.

"We're just peeking around this corner," I whispered back. "Be ready to run if we have to."

I inched forward. The last shelf held bottles of laundry detergent, and I peeked over the tops of the bottles.

Now I had a glimpse of one of the major streets of Refuge City. I'd lost track of what time it might be. Was it nine? Ten? Eleven o'clock at night? But even if it was later than that— even if it was the middle of the night—the street should have been full of cars and trucks and taxis. The sidewalks should have been full of wanderers out for a show or a sports game or just a walk. This was Refuge City!

The street looked empty and dark. The sidewalk looked empty and dark.

Then I heard a slight whistling noise, and something big—a boulder? A TV? An office chair like the one Enu had thrown?—came sailing toward another plate-glass window. I hunched over, braced for another crash.

It didn't happen. The giant object dissolved in midair, leaving behind nothing but traces of ash that fell to the ground like spent firecrackers. Moments later, a light went on over a second-floor balcony on the opposite side of the street. Two Enforcers in dark uniforms stood over a huddled shape.

"That man threw his patio table down at the Enforcers," Enu whispered in my ear. "And the Enforcers vaporized it and were there to catch him two seconds later."

Enu sounded like he wanted me to tell him he was wrong, that that wasn't what had happened. He wanted me to make him understand what he'd just seen in an entirely different way.

In an entirely safe and peaceful way.

But Enu was right. And the Enforcers on the balcony weren't the only danger: Now my eyes could pick out a small group of Enforcers patrolling the dark street in front of the Emporium of Food. They were close enough to hear Enu and me if we raised our voices to a shout—or maybe even just a normal speaking level.

Though, what did I know about Enforcers' ears? What if they had superhuman hearing and could detect our whispering?

My fingers itched to reach for my phone and look it up. Of course I'd looked up everything I could about the Enforcers last night, when Edwy and I had first found out that Enforcers had arrested Rosi back in Cursed Town, back in our parents' hometown. Last night, nobody had known much of anything. The Internet had been full of rumors, with only kernels of confirmed fact here and there. And though I'd bragged to Edwy about hacking into the Enforcers' own online network, that had been a painstaking process, requiring lots of trial and error (and *dangerous* errors) for every small crumb of success.

But last night, Cursed Town was the *only* place on the planet where Enforcers had taken control. Surely now that they were everywhere on Earth, the online world was full of information. . . .

Enu dug his fingers into my arm and hissed into my ear, "Did you see that?"

My gaze snapped back to the Enforcers and the huddled shape of the one solitary rebellious man on the balcony across the street.

The Enforcers were kicking the man in the stomach. They were kicking him *hard*.

"But that's—that's not—" I stammered. "He deserves a trial. He's innocent until proven guilty. He—No matter what he did, he . . ."

"That isn't how Refuge City handles criminals," Enu whispered, and in spite of myself I admired the way he could boil down everything that was swirling in my brain into seven words.

Refuge City had no prisons. It didn't even have jails. People were banished from the city forever if they broke any of the truly serious laws.

And no one who had earned the right to live in Refuge City wanted to be banished. So of course no one broke any major laws.

"Do you think—" I began whispering to Enu. But before I could say another word, he tightened his grip on my arm. It seemed entirely possible he would snap my arm bone in two.

"Shh!" he hissed in my ear. "Do you hear—"

I slid my hand over his mouth, because if he was going to tell me not to talk, he shouldn't talk either.

I listened to the darkness around us so hard that my ears rang. Out on the street, the patrolling Enforcers stepped silently, their loud marching from earlier in the day replaced by stealth and sneakiness. That made them even more dangerous.

But I can still see the same cluster of five patrolling

Enforcers I saw a moment ago. Nothing's changed there. I don't have to worry about them any more than I did a moment ago. . . .

Even the two Enforcers kicking the man up on the balcony did their terrible deed in silence. Maybe the man had passed out from the pain.

I couldn't watch *that*. I looked back to the Enforcers on the street. There *had* been only five of them earlier, right? Surely there was no way I'd missed seeing one or two or three others in the shadows, and those others were now patrolling *inside* the Emporium of Food. . . .

I struggled so hard to talk myself into feeling certain that there weren't any extra Enforcers. I wanted to believe it so much.

Because now I could hear the same faint sound that Enu was warning me about.

Footsteps. Behind us.

Coming our way.

CHAPTER SIX

Enu pointed left and I pointed right, and without words, it was impossible to explain my strategy: *No, no, of course any Enforcer would expect us to run* away *from the window and the street. We've got to out-think them and outsmart them and act completely unpredictable or they'll catch us right away. . . .*

If they caught us, would they start beating us the same way they were beating the man on the balcony?

Enu tugged on my arm, and I tugged on his, and I felt so light-headed, I wasn't sure I could run anywhere anyway. Maybe I would just faint. Maybe I would just vomit, and that's how the Enforcers would catch us.

"Enu? Kiandra?" someone whispered.

I whirled around, and—

It was Edwy. No, Edwy and Rosi both, tiptoeing toward us, clutching each other's arms like they were holding each other up, daring each other to be brave.

"Are you trying to get killed?" I demanded. "Are you trying to get us *all* killed?"

I barely remembered to keep my voice down, to contain my outrage in a whisper.

"We were worried about you," Edwy whispered back.

"Yeah, and if we'd been in trouble, what were you going to do about it?" Enu snarled.

In the darkness they both sounded so young. Like little boys arguing, their chests puffed out like miniature roosters. I wanted to roll my eyes at Rosi and complain, *Boys and their egos* . . . I wanted this to be about nothing more serious than making fun of my brothers.

"We're fine," I whispered. "But there are Enforcers right over there. . . ."

I pointed past the shelf. Any normal kid would have understood that I meant, *Stay away! Go back now!* But I kept forgetting that Edwy and Rosi weren't normal.

Both of them stepped up to the gap in the shelf full of laundry detergent bottles. Both of them peeked over top of the bottles. Rosi gasped, and Edwy grabbed Enu and me and yanked us closer.

"They're hurting that man!" Rosi cried, and she seemed to be having as much trouble as I had keeping her voice down. "Somebody has to stop them!"

I threw my arm across her chest, holding her back.

"Oh no," I said. "You are not running out there to help. It won't do any good. They'll just start beating you, too."

I saw that Enu had mirrored my action, grabbing Edwy's shoulders too.

"But we have to do something!" Rosi protested.

Something wet touched the crook of my elbow. She was crying.

Edwy's hand brushed my arm. He was reaching out to Rosi too.

"This isn't Fredtown," he whispered to her. "You would have gone running off to help, there. But here . . ."

"Here it's even more important!" Rosi hissed back.

She struggled against my grip.

"No, no—we have to be smart about helping," Edwy whispered.

Rosi stopped struggling so hard.

"Tell me how," she begged.

"We can't overpower those Enforcers," Enu contributed, leaning in close, practically touching his head to mine and Edwy's. "We don't have any power at all."

It was heartbreaking to hear Enu admit that. Enu normally acted like he had power and control over everyone and everything.

"If the Freds found out this was happening . . . ," Edwy began.

Rosi shook her head frantically.

"The Freds are obeying the rules," she said bitterly. "They'll abide by every edict and proclamation of the intergalactic court. And the intergalactic court says Freds aren't allowed on Earth anymore. But the Enforcers have the right to be here. To do whatever they want. That's the agreement."

"Then we have to get the intergalactic court to change its mind," Edwy said. "If *they* saw this . . ."

I had nothing to contribute. As far as I could tell, this was a pointless conversation. And a dangerous one. What if the Enforcers outside could hear our hissing and whispering? What if they were right this minute creeping our way?

I kept my grip on Rosi's shoulders, but I moved my head forward, to scan the streetscape once more.

The Enforcers had stopped beating and kicking the man on the balcony. They'd balanced his unconscious body over the railing, as though they planned to come back later and scoop him up. (That is, if he didn't fall over first.) They'd moved on to another balcony, more directly in my sightlines. Now they were beating a woman and a little boy.

I turned my body sideways, because Rosi really shouldn't see this.

But Edwy grabbed my arm, tugging it forward.

"Kiandra can help," he said. "Kiandra can record everything the Enforcers are doing on her phone. And then she can send the video to the intergalactic court without the Enforcers even knowing. She knows how to do that. She can hack into any system! She can do anything with computers!"

He had such pride in his voice. Such pride in *me*. I didn't think he was right—I didn't think there was any way to stop the Enforcers. But Rosi started tugging on my arm too.

"That . . . might help," she whispered through her tears. "It won't stop the Enforcers from hurting these people, but it could stop them from hurting anyone else. . . ."

"That would show them!" Enu agreed.

I thought about the snippet of TV news Enu and I had seen—how the Enforcers' general was telling the world that their invasion had been a peaceful "rescue," that everybody wanted them here.

No—he wasn't just telling the world, everyone on Planet Earth, I realized. *The Enforcers don't care what people on Earth think or believe. That's what the general was telling the* universe. *That was their lie to the intergalactic court. The intergalactic court needs to see the truth. And I can show them.*

I knew the risks. I didn't know much about the intergalactic court—maybe they wouldn't even care. Maybe they already knew what the Enforcers were like. But I couldn't let them pretend they didn't know—or let the Freds on the intergalactic court pretend they were all saintly and good. Enu's words woke up something deep inside me, something that had been numb ever since I'd seen that Dumpster vaporized. I was Kiandra Watanaboneset, and I might be about to die, but I wasn't going to die for nothing. If I had to die, I was going to die trying.

I had a purpose.

My hand curled around the familiar curve of my mobile phone. I pulled it out of my pocket, turned it on, and aimed it at the pair of Enforcers looming over the woman and the little boy. I hit the record button just as one of the Enforcers smashed his fist into the woman's face.

A split second later, the phone was yanked from my hand.

CHAPTER SEVEN

I peered around frantically, because I hadn't seen or heard anyone approaching us; Enu, Edwy, and Rosi hadn't called out any warnings.

The phone had been yanked straight *up*, and I could see it hovering right over my head, but no hand held it. It was just suspended in midair.

"Run!" Enu gasped.

But before any of us could move, a wide beam of light spun toward us. Was it possible to brace yourself to be vaporized?

It took me a moment to realize: This wasn't that kind of light. This light caught us in its glow, but it didn't hurt us; it didn't destroy us.

Enu banged into the outer edge of the glow and fell to the floor.

"The light is . . . a cage," Rosi whispered. "We're trapped."

I could see her clearly now: the rips in her tuniclike dress, the tear streaks on her cheeks, the desert dust still layered in her dark hair. I remembered that she was a wanted fugitive, that the Enforcers had condemned her to a life in prison for supposedly starting a battle in Cursed Town. She was actually innocent of anything except wanting to help Edwy—and escaping from the Enforcers twice.

It was hopeless to think that the Enforcers wouldn't figure out who she was—or that they wouldn't figure out who all four of us were. But I still moved to the edge of the light and screamed, "Let us go! We haven't done anything wrong!"

"Our parents could bribe—" Enu began, but I held a finger to my lips and he stopped.

"When we don't come back, Ze—" Edwy started.

My hand shot out and slammed over his mouth.

"Don't say any names," I warned. "I'm sure they can hear everything we say."

Edwy pushed my hand away.

"I won't say names, but *she'll* help," he said. "And if she goes to her parents, they will too."

Rosi silently mouthed a single name: *Bobo*. The tears welled in her eyes again.

"*He's* safe," I whispered.

I wanted to say I was absolutely certain that Bobo, Zeba, and Cana would stay safe, that the identity blocking I'd done would keep them protected. But just talking about them would endanger them. Unless . . .

"I hope they catch those other kids we were with, too!" I said, throwing all my bitterness and fear into my voice. "After they betrayed us and said they wanted to help the Enforcers—I hate them!"

Rosi's eyes widened and her tears flooded out now. She didn't understand my doublespeak, the way having me say the other kids were on the Enforcers' side might help them if there were caught. I guess her Fredtown childhood hadn't prepared her for interpreting even blatant lies. But Edwy gripped her shoulder, and I saw: He understood.

So stop stereotyping and thinking all the Fredtown kids are alike, I told myself.

What if all the Enforcers weren't alike either? All we needed was to convince even one of them to let us go.

"Please!" I called out into the darkness again. "Set us free!"

Caught in the light, I could barely see what was happening beyond. But none of the Enforcers out in the street turned around. The Enforcers on the balcony above finished beating the woman and little boy and moved out of sight.

"They can't hear us," I said in disgust, sagging to the floor beside Enu.

"But before, you said . . ." Enu squinted at me in confusion. "Does this mean we can say anything we—"

"Oh, I'm sure *somebody's* eavesdropping on us," I said. "Even recording us. But the Enforcers out there, the people out there—they can't." I gestured toward the street. "There's some sort of soundproofing that goes along with this special light. I bet . . . I bet that's why we couldn't hear the people on the balconies screaming. The ones the Enforcers were beating. That was soundproofed too."

Enu gazed vacantly at me. But Edwy crouched beside me.

"You're figuring out how this works," he said quietly. "Can you figure out how to escape?"

"Um . . ."

I wanted to live up to his faith in me. I looked down at the floor. Could Enu dig a tunnel out with his bare hands?

No, as soon as we opened any part of the floor, the light would seep down into the hole. We need darkness. We need . . .

Just then, the light around us jerked to the side and then rose into the air. Incredibly, we rose with it. My mobile phone, out of reach a moment earlier, clunked me on the head. It was falling, falling. . . .

I thrust out my hand and grabbed the phone just before it could fall past my feet.

"That's evidence against you," Edwy hissed.

"It's evidence against the Enforcers, too," I whispered stubbornly back to him, as I tucked the phone into my shorts pocket once again.

I'm not sure I was being logical. Maybe it just felt good to hold the phone in my hand. Maybe it made me feel like myself again, to have it in my pocket.

The light beam we were trapped in lifted us past the broken windows of the Emporium of Food and out into the street. It shifted shape: One moment it felt like we were in a globe of light; the next, improbably, we were in a square. Our square of light settled into place a good nine or ten meters above the ground. Peering out into the darkness around us, I could see others above and below and beside us: people lying on the ground, then lying in midair nine meters up, then again eighteen meters up, then maybe twenty-seven or thirty. . . . Maybe to all of them—to the ones who were conscious, anyway—it seemed like *they* were the ones trapped in squares of light, and *we* were trapped in darkness.

Either way, we were all trapped.

Just moments earlier I'd been thinking about how Refuge City had never needed a prison or a jail. Not in its entire history. Not under human rule. But the Enforcers had taken over mere hours ago, and they'd already set up the first prison: an odd one with invisible bars.

And Enu, Edwy, Rosi, and I were locked inside.

CHAPTER EIGHT

Enu battered his shoulders against the sides of the square of light. He jumped up and down, as if that was a way to break through. On alternate bounces, he raised his arms high over his head and shoved his hands against the ceiling.

The other three of us just watched. If he couldn't break out with all his muscles, none of the rest of us could either.

Finally he collapsed to the floor of our bizarre prison cell.

"This is hopeless," he moaned. He narrowed his eyes to slits. "It's all your fault, Kiandra. You *knew* it was dangerous to turn your phone on. You told me it wasn't even safe to watch TV, and yet you linked to the Internet? I told you you were addicted!"

"I didn't link to anything!" I protested. "All I did was hit record! You idiot, don't you know it's possible to turn on the video function on a phone without linking to the Internet?"

I felt guilty enough without Enu blaming me too.

"This is my fault," Rosi whispered. She slumped to the

floor with the rest of us. "I'm the one who insisted we had to do something."

"You think the Enforcers have some device to detect any time they're being recorded?" Edwy asked. "You think that's how they figured out we were there?"

I liked that he wasn't just sitting around moaning and groaning and regretting things that couldn't be changed, like Enu and Rosi were.

I also liked that his analysis made it seem even more likely that Zeba, Bobo, and Cana were safe, and would stay safe.

"That's what makes the most sense to me," I told Edwy.

"Or the Enforcers were just playing with us all along, like a cat does with a mouse," Enu muttered. "Like, they tracked us from the moment we got out of Udans's truck, and they just didn't bother scooping us up until now."

Don't say Udans's name, I wanted to snarl at Enu. *Don't let Rosi know how likely it is that the Enforcers could snatch up the other three kids too.*

But I also wanted to say, *Don't talk about cats and mice.*

For the past several years, Enu and I had lived on the top floor of one of Refuge City's swankiest apartment building. *We'd* never had to worry about mice. The only mice I'd ever seen had been in science-experiment videos and at pet stores, during that brief phase when I was a stupid little girl who thought having a cuddly animal around would give me someone to love. (Or . . .

someone who would love me.) It turned out that Enu was allergic to everything with fur, so I'd ended up with a salamander for a week. Not exactly cuddly, not even fun, just a nuisance to remember to feed. So I took it back. After that, we never had anything but virtual pets. And I let Enu convince me that it was more interesting to see how quickly we could get the virtual three-toed Samutis and the virtual four-eyed Gonzas to die, rather than keeping them alive and happy.

Yeah, Enu and I had messed-up childhoods.

But *real* cats and *real* mice . . . the only reason either of us knew anything about them was because of our parents' stories about their own childhoods back in Cursed Town. The war had started in Cursed Town when I was only a baby; I'd barely turned one when our parents had had Udans smuggle us into Refuge City. I had no memory of my mother or father hugging me, of either of them tucking us into bed at night. I knew my parents' faces only from computer screens, from their remote calls after the war ended and Cursed Town got sporadic Internet connection again.

When I was little, I *loved* those calls. I'd reached for my parents' faces on the screen, and I'd hung on to their every word about a delightful, rustic place that sounded so different from big, noisy, overwhelming Refuge City. I sobbed every time one of those calls ended.

Then I found out what had really happened in Cursed

Town—all the killings, all the betrayals, all the deceit. I found out about my own parents' guilt, buried deep beneath innocent stories about picking flowers in the meadow and roasting marshmallows over an open flame.

Now I *despised* my parents. I hated everything about them, everything about Cursed Town. Everything I'd ever longed for and loved as a small child.

And the war in Cursed Town had been the final straw for humanity. It was the reason the Freds had come in and started taking away human babies.

So, indirectly, it was the reason the Enforcers were here now. It was the reason Enu, Edwy, Rosi, and I were locked in this bizarre cage with hundreds of others.

Everything was my parents' fault.

So, okay, now that you've figured that out—what are you going to do about it?

Nothing. There was nothing any of us *could* do.

Rosi had started crying again, and Edwy patted her awkwardly on the shoulder.

"We'll be fine," he told her. "*Everyone* will be fine. Things will work out. You'll see."

I guess lying ran in our family.

I put my hands over my ears and huddled against the wall. I didn't think I could sleep—how was that even possible at a time and in a place like this? But at least I could pretend.

Just as I touched it, the wall of our prison cell quivered. It slid forward; in fact, the whole cell slid forward and up. The cells around us moved too. It was like all the cells were on a conveyor belt now—or maybe a roller coaster. Enu loved roller coasters, and Refuge City's amusement parks had a lot of them. There had been a time when I always went with him. I recognized this creaky inching forward from all those hot summer days when we sat in a roller-coaster car creeping up a steep hill.

I braced myself for the inevitable plunge.

"They're taking us somewhere!" Edwy cried excitedly. "Maybe it's, like, a courtroom! And they'll let us explain. . . ."

"Only one of us should do the talking," Rosi said.

Maybe she was wilier than I'd thought. She clearly meant that if only one of us spoke, there was no danger of us getting our stories crossed.

"Kiandra, it should be you," Edwy said.

His green eyes glowed, wide and trusting.

Wait a minute—am I the one he trusts the most?

Automatically I glanced at Enu, because surely he would protest. Surely he would say, *I'm the big brother. I'm the biggest. Those Enforcers will regret messing with me!*

But Enu had his head down, like he was studying his shoelaces. Or trying not to vomit.

Maybe Enu was even more terrified than I was?

We kept rising, higher, higher, higher. After only a few moments we were looking *down* on the skyscrapers of Refuge

City. They were so far below, their lights were muted and dim. Panic bubbled in my gut. Every human instinct I had screamed that this was *wrong*. Nobody should be able to look so far down through nothingness. When you were a hundred stories up in the sky, you needed a real floor below you. You needed a *hundred* floors beneath you. Ones that were completely solid and visible. Not see-through.

Beside me, Enu began to gag.

"Don't look," I told him. "Close your eyes."

I couldn't bear to turn my head the other direction, to see how Edwy and Rosi were faring. I had to keep looking straight out, or *I* would vomit.

Suddenly our prison cell jerked to a stop. I'd thought we'd gone higher than any skyscraper, but I was wrong. Out of the corner of my eye, I could see a man standing on what appeared to be yet another balcony, on the highest floor of some building I didn't recognize.

Or, no—it was an Enforcer. The faint outline of his bubble-shaped helmet glinted in the moonlight. He held his body so stiffly, so unnaturally, that it seemed he wasn't used to existing in a human shape. Or maybe he wanted to seem entirely imperious, entirely unapproachable.

Another prison cell hovered between us and the Enforcer. I could just barely make out the shapes inside the cell of a woman and a man clutching a baby and a toddler. I couldn't hear any sound coming from that prison cell, but you could tell the two children were wailing; you could tell the parents were throwing themselves prostrate before the Enforcer and begging for mercy.

The Enforcer didn't seem to hear them either. He jerked his arm to the right, and the prison cell ahead of us spun off in that direction.

And then it vanished.

"Will that—will that happen to us?" Edwy stammered. "Kiandra, Enu, please, you have to—"

Whatever Edwy was begging us to do was lost as our prison cell jerked forward, and Edwy slammed against the wall.

Now we were the ones directly in front of the Enforcer on the balcony.

"Please," I moaned. Without even thinking about it, I'd cupped my hands into a prayerful pose. "Please don't—"

The Enforcer slashed his arm to the left.

It was left, not right! My brain screamed. *Maybe that's better?*

But our prison cell spun away just as quickly as the other one had.

How was I supposed to prepare to be vaporized?

Strangely, my last thought was, *Our mother and father will be so sad when they hear that all their children died.*

And then the light around me vanished, and so did everything else.

CHAPTER NINE

We didn't die.

At least, I didn't *think* we'd died.

I opened my eyes to more darkness, and to the disorienting sense that I might have been unconscious for five minutes or five years—there was no way for me to tell.

On either side of me, Enu and Edwy were stirring. I heard groans. Was it just them, or was Rosi there on the other side of Edwy, waking up too?

I lifted my head to look, and then I was the one moaning in misery. The movement woke up my nerve endings; my head felt like it had been battered against solid concrete for hours on end. For all I knew, maybe it had been.

So the Enforcer didn't want us dead; he just wanted to make us wish we were dead?

I was stubborn. I made myself sit up anyway.

My head was so woozy I almost passed out again. But wherever we were now, we still had moonlight. I could see another dim shape beyond Edwy's groaning body. Rosi was turning her head side to side, passing her hand in front of her face, just as slow and logy as the rest of us.

I had to prop myself up on my elbows to keep from falling. My arms felt bloated and heavy; it felt like I was moving elephant legs. I glanced back, the motion making my head throb harder. But my arms *looked* like they always did, as skinny as ever.

"What happened? Where are we?" Edwy groaned.

"Not . . . not in Refuge City anymore," I mumbled back to him. There weren't any buildings in sight. We weren't lying on concrete or asphalt. "Are we . . . back in the desert?"

Painstakingly, I drew my fingers toward the palms of my hands. But my fingertips didn't brush against sand. They inched across hard, crusted-over dirt. Dirt so solid, not even a single blade of grass poked through.

"We've got to go back," Rosi moaned. "We have to get back to Refuge City and find . . . the others." She turned her head toward me, and I could almost see her deciding that she wasn't worried about Enforcers hearing her now. "Bobo will be so scared. . . ."

"How are we going to do that when we don't even know where we are?" Enu demanded. "When we're out here totally alone?"

Maybe only I could hear the panic in his voice. Maybe

Edwy and Rosi thought he was just being mean.

"The Freds told us people can navigate by the stars at night," Rosi whimpered. "If anyone knows what to look for . . . That's what I tried to do out in the desert. . . ."

I expected Enu to erupt: *The stars? That's stupid! That only works if you know what direction you want to go! And if we don't know where we are, we don't know which way it is back to Refuge City!* But before he could speak, I said quickly, "Or I could use the GPS on my phone. We don't have to worry about the Enforcers finding us now, since they're the ones who sent us here."

Eagerly, I pulled out my phone. I kept myself propped on one arm—I seemed to need that. Still, if anyone could operate a phone one-handed, it was me. I pressed my thumb against the screen to bypass the security code, and then clicked into a mapping app.

The screen stayed blank, searching for a connection.

I struggled to keep breathing normally.

"I guess maybe we're too far out," I said finally. I kept my hand curved around the phone like it was a security blanket. I tried to keep my voice nonchalant, like I really didn't care. "I guess it's too far to the nearest cell tower, or . . ."

My voice trembled. But, strangely, none of the others seemed to be listening. They all had their heads tilted back; all three of them gazed up as if they were taking Rosi seriously, and seeking guidance from above.

Enu laid a shaking hand on my shoulder and pointed off into the distance, toward the sky.

"Am I just seeing double?" he asked. "Tell me I'm just seeing double. My eyes haven't adjusted yet. . . ."

"Or did the Enforcers bring an extra moon with them?" Edwy asked. "Or is that their spaceship hovering overhead, and it just *looks* like the moon? There can't be two!"

Two moons? What were they even talking about? I wanted to make fun of them for hallucinating, for trusting their own groggy eyes so soon after waking. They were probably both still dreaming.

But I looked up, and they were right. Two moons hung low in the sky, both somewhere between half and full, both so luminous and bright that I could see the pockmarks on their faces. The pockmarks weren't the same; the moons weren't identical. They weren't mirrored images, either. So Enu was wrong about the double vision.

And both moons were definitely moons, not spaceships.

So . . . next theory? I wondered.

Rosi cleared her throat.

"Or," she whispered, "do those two moons mean . . . we're on another planet, in another solar system? Again?"

CHAPTER TEN

"**The Enforcers could send** us to another planet that easily?" Enu asked numbly. "Just with a swipe of the one guy's arm?"

"Rosi, didn't you say Mrs. Osemwe told you there were different ways to travel between planets?" Edwy asked. "When all of us Fredtown kids came back to Earth, we thought we were just on an airplane, but they were fooling us. That means . . ."

I stopped listening to Edwy and his theories. I didn't even bother asking who Mrs. Osemwe was.

We're not in Refuge City anymore. We're not even on Earth.

I couldn't stop staring at the two moons.

"How are we ever going to get back to Bobo now?" Rosi wailed.

My brain skipped ahead to other questions: *How can we survive in a place that can't even grow grass? Where there aren't any buildings or cities? Where there's no way to walk or drive or ride back to Refuge City—not without a spaceship? Or . . . whatever the Enforcer used?*

I made myself stand up. I wanted to get away from the others' moaning and groaning—and from the questions in my own mind. But if propping myself up into a seated position had been hard, standing felt a hundred times more precarious. My legs wobbled; my knees threatened to buckle. I felt again like I was on an amusement-park ride—the centrifuge type, the kind that made your limbs feel unbearably heavy.

"Gravity," I grunted. "I think this is a planet with stronger gravity."

I fell over, bashing my knee against a clod of dirt.

A moment too late Edwy reached out to catch me.

"Oh, *weird*," he said, watching his own arms draw back in slow motion. "Sorry, Kiandra. I thought I could help."

I'd seen video of astronauts walking on the moon—Earth's moon, I mean. They leaped and bounced, even in heavy-looking spacesuits. Because the moon has less gravity than the Earth. But this was the opposite effect. I felt pinned to the ground.

Was it possible the air was thicker too?

"Are you hurt?" Rosi asked.

"Just my pride," I muttered.

Rosi shot me a confused look—oh, yeah, kids raised in Fredtown probably didn't get the concept of pride. But then she tilted her head to the side and said, "It makes sense that this planet would have stronger gravity, if it can hold on to more moons than Earth can. And don't they both look bigger than Earth's moon? Or is that just because they're low in the sky right now?"

My hands itched to look this up online, to see if she was right or not.

"School stuff," Edwy snorted. "That's the kind of thing teachers would want us figuring out."

"Yeah," Enu agreed. Of course my two school-hating brothers would be in solidarity on this. "Why does that matter? Who cares?"

"I'm trying to figure out everything I can," Rosi said in a small voice, as if the two boys had hurt her. "Maybe figuring out one thing can lead to figuring out other things. Like . . ."

"Why are we here?" I finished for her. "Why did the Enforcer *send* us here?"

"We're not going to find that out lying around on the ground talking," Enu scoffed. "If the light is gone, I bet we aren't trapped in a cage anymore. Which means . . ."

He rose to a crawling position, then stood and took a cautious step away from the rest of us. Enu would tell anyone who listened what a great athlete he was, but on this planet even he moved like an overweight gorilla.

"See?" he said. He waved—or, more accurately, slow-motion *flopped*—his arms in front of him. He reached farther out than where the boundaries of our light cage had once stood. "We can escape."

"Because probably the whole planet's a prison," I muttered. I swayed, feeling light-headed all over again. Instantly I wanted to take back my own words.

What if I was right? What if this planet *was* a prison?

Or worse—a graveyard?

Enu took another step forward. Suddenly, as if he'd triggered it, a beam of blinding light shot toward us from a single pole we hadn't been able to see before, off in the distance. I heard a door scrape open behind us.

"Took you long enough to wake up," a deep, evil-sounding voice complained. "And three of you are as scrawny as eels. . . . Are you *children*? They sent us children? What good is that?"

"We're good kids," Rosi said faintly.

The evil voice broke off for an evil chuckle; then it replied, "I'll beat that out of you."

The light we were caught in swung past us, like a guard tower's searchlight. For only a moment the glow struck the shadowy figure in the doorway of what appeared to be a concrete box. The creature was gargantuan, and it was hard to say which were more threatening: his bulging muscles or the guns and grenades he wore strapped across his chest and hips.

If this planet was a prison, this creature was our prison guard.

CHAPTER ELEVEN

"He's not wearing a helmet," Edwy whispered.

The guard's face was in the shadows, but there was enough of a glow around him to see that this was true: He had no protective bubble surrounding his head.

Instinctively, my hand clenched around the clod of dirt I'd hit my knee on. Back in the desert, back on Earth, we'd had our short-lived victory against the Enforcers because they hadn't learned to wear helmets yet. From his hiding place in a cave, Udans had managed to throw rock after rock at the small cluster of Enforcers sent out to chase Rosi. He'd knocked open the masks that made them look human; *that* had knocked them unconscious, because they couldn't breathe in Earth's atmosphere without a mask or a helmet.

Could I use this clod of dirt the way Udans had used a rock? Or, if I couldn't, could I transfer it quickly enough to Enu and let him throw it?

Would he think to take the stronger gravity into account

before he sent the clod sailing off toward the prison guard's face? What were the odds that he could hit the guard in the right section of the mask—before the guard shot us all?

No, maybe, probably not, the chances against it are about infinity to one. . . .

How could I even think about Udans's feat without also thinking about how that had probably sealed his fate?

Could I think about any of that without falling over in grief?

The guard let out another evil chuckle, a sound like the tolling of doom.

"I can hear you, you know," he said.

He didn't seem the least bit worried about anyone hurling anything at his face.

"My brother, this little boy—he just . . . he just likes to think out loud," I said quickly. "He talks all the time about everything he sees."

I wanted to elbow Edwy, to get him to start babbling senselessly: *The sky is dark; this planet has two moons; I'm wearing a blue shirt. . . .* It was a lesson I'd learned from hacking: The best way to cover your tracks was to create lots and lots of tracks, too many for anyone to follow.

Would it be too obvious if *I* started babbling like that?

Before I could decide, the guard snorted, a sound at least as awful as his chuckles.

"Swatting away little gnats like you can be so annoying," he growled. "So I'll tell you: This planet has an atmosphere that both your species and mine can breathe. None of us need masks or helmets. Not you *or* me. Or, I should say, the atmosphere doesn't harm me, and it is only *minimally* poisonous to humans. So you won't die until after you've served your purpose here."

I shivered, but Edwy was incredibly bold.

"What *is* our purpose here?" he asked.

"Hey! *I* ask the questions!" the guard shouted. He swiped an arm to the right, and Edwy's head slammed into me— exactly as if he'd been punched on the side of his face and he'd had no chance to brace himself for the impact.

Edwy rubbed his face.

"How'd he do that from way over there?" he mumbled.

Edwy's head jerked back, his head bouncing off Rosi's shoulder this time. Now it was like he'd been punched in the nose.

"Anyone else got any questions?" the guard taunted.

"N-n-no," Rosi stammered. She put her arms around Edwy and whispered, "Please, Edwy, don't ask anything else. This isn't a Fred-teacher. He isn't going to be nice."

That was the understatement of the century.

I remembered how much my older brother hated anyone telling him what to do. I swiveled toward Enu, but he was just standing there frozen, as terrified as I was.

The guard yawned. I heard his jaw crack. Or whatever Enforcers had instead of jaws.

"It's ten hours to sunrise," he said. "Overnight temperatures out here this time of year can dip down to—oh, I don't know what primitive numbering system you humans use. Think of the coldest temperature you've ever heard of, and then imagine it a hundred times worse. If you can. *I* don't care if you all freeze to death out here tonight, but central command gets touchy about spending time and effort to send prisoners out here if I don't get *some* work out of them."

"We're prisoners?" Rosi murmured. "And you're going to make us work? For you?"

Edwy lunged toward her, as if he wanted to take whatever invisible punch was headed her way for asking questions. But the guard didn't do anything to beat her up from a distance.

Maybe he didn't even recognize her words as questions.

Maybe he thought she was just accepting reality.

"Into your cage," the guard said. "Now."

And then I felt the oddest sensation: It was like somebody else's brain took over my body. My legs unbent; my torso rose; my sandaled feet rolled into position. I felt the heels, then the balls of my feet, then my toes propel me forward, left foot, then right, then left again. I wanted to look down to see how my feet were moving without my control, but I couldn't bend my neck. Somebody else—the guard?—was forcing my eyes to stay trained straight ahead, looking only toward the doorway of the concrete box.

Did my limbs feel like elephant legs to whoever was moving them now?

The guard stepped to the side as we neared the door. I wanted so badly to turn my head and stare at him, to see close up if any part of his body was vulnerable, if there was any place we could kick or punch to overpower *him*. There were four of us and only one of him—wasn't that an advantage?

But I couldn't turn my head any more than I could bend my neck. My head stayed facing forward; my legs kept marching, out of my control.

I couldn't do anything except what the Enforcer wanted me to do.

And think, I reminded myself. *I can still think.*

CHAPTER
TWELVE

The doorway we entered led to dark, squalid stairs. The steps were uneven—haphazard, even—and it was terrifying not to have any control over how fast we climbed down. My brain screamed, *I'm going to trip! I'm going to fall!* But I couldn't open my mouth to beg, *Please! Let us go slower!* I couldn't even groan. My vocal cords were just as frozen as my mouth, as my tongue, as my neck.

We reached the bottom and there was no light here. I couldn't see Enu ahead of me; I was incapable of turning my neck to see Edwy and Rosi behind me. I couldn't even call out to make sure they were there. My legs kept propelling me forward. Then, abruptly, my body pivoted to the left. I heard a clanging behind me.

"Good night," the guard's voice taunted from high above us.

And then suddenly I tumbled to the ground, my face hitting Enu's heel.

"Get off me!" he yelled, shoving me away. "Let me go!"

"Enu, stop!" I cried. "I'm not doing anything! The Enforcer just . . . gave us back control of our own bodies!"

"Finally!" he grunted.

"I never want that to happen again," Edwy moaned behind me. "That was awful. I couldn't even control my own body enough to sneeze, and I needed to sneeze so bad. . . ."

"So sneeze now," Enu growled at him.

"I . . . can't," Edwy said. "Don't need to anymore."

"Is everyone okay?" Rosi asked.

I slid my hands over my arms and legs, as if I needed to reassure myself they were truly mine again. I was a little surprised that they didn't feel any different than usual. I even seemed to have adjusted to the stronger gravity of this planet. Or, at least, the gravity seemed like a minor problem now, compared with the Enforcer's power over us.

"How did the Enforcer do that?" I asked.

"How do we fight it?" Edwy countered.

"Maybe if we negotiate . . . ," Rosi began.

"No, we fight," Enu said. "We fight this to the death. We kill every Enforcer we can."

"How are you going to do that when just one Enforcer can make all four of us walk down into a dark cage any time he wants?" I asked.

Instantly I wished I hadn't opened my mouth. Because

that question lingered in the darkness. No one answered me. Nobody could.

"Maybe we should just get some sleep," Rosi finally said. "Maybe we can figure out something in the morning. Should . . . should we all huddle together for warmth?"

"I guess so," Edwy agreed.

Enu and I didn't say anything, but we all scooted close together. My head sagged onto Enu's shoulder; he leaned against my arm. I couldn't quite remember it, but this might have been how we'd slept when we'd first arrived in Refuge City as toddlers, torn away from our parents and the only home we'd ever known.

Edwy and Rosi leaned against my other side. I thought about how much better it had made me feel to have Cana's hand in mine, back in the basement in Refuge City.

"We need to make sure our hands don't get cold either," I said, lacing the fingers of my right hand in Enu's left, my left hand in Edwy's right.

And this is how desperate we all were: My brothers let me hold their hands.

CHAPTER
THIRTEEN

The buzzing of an alarm woke us. We were still surrounded by total darkness, so I had no way of knowing if morning had arrived or if the guard was waking us up in the middle of the night. But I'd barely had a chance to stretch out my stiff arms and legs when suddenly my body stood up, seemingly entirely on its own.

"Wha—" Enu began, before his voice was silenced and he shoved away from me and rose to his feet as well.

Okay, pay attention, I told myself. *The Enforcer didn't take us over all at once. So maybe . . . it takes a lot of effort? A lot of energy?*

My body began moving toward the wall. I could hear Enu, Edwy, and Rosi shuffling alongside me. Then suddenly the top half of my body plunged forward, bent over at the waist. My chin and mouth landed in something slimy and cold. My mouth opened, my teeth chewed, my throat swallowed the nastiest food I'd ever tasted.

Cold porridge? I thought. *Gruel?*

I only knew those terms from stories. Back when Enu and I were little, one of our worst nannies had always threatened to feed us gruel. But even she had never done it.

Now here we were, all four of us gobbling down disgusting swill, burying our faces in it to eat like horses. Or pigs.

The minute I have control again, I told myself, *I'm going to scream out, "We're humans, not animals! Humans use* silverware! *Or chopsticks! We're civilized!"*

My tongue licked the bottom of the rough wooden tray.

I could get a splinter! I wanted to scream. *I could cut my tongue and start dripping blood everywhere!*

My tongue kept licking the wood, hunting down the last nasty, crusted-on grain.

Then my waist unbent; my spine straightened up. I could feel a line of slobber and gruel slithering down my chin, and all I wanted to do was wipe it off. But my elbow wouldn't bend. I concentrated hard, and . . .

I managed to swing the fingers of my right hand ever so slightly to the left.

Of course, this was pointless if whatever force controlling my body wouldn't let me lift my hand to my face.

But it's good to know, I thought. *This proves the Enforcer doesn't control everything. Right now all he cares about is making me walk.*

And making me feel like I didn't have control.

The four of us climbed the stairs, and Rosi, who was in the lead, pushed the door open. Through a thick haze I could see the first rays of sunrise shining on a vast, empty plain: nothing but dirt and rock. Even with more light than the night before, I couldn't see a single blade of grass, a single sign that anything grew here.

Or that anyone lived here.

"The mines," a voice sounded beside me. "Where you'll work the rest of your lives."

No, no, no, no . . . , my brain screamed.

"Dig!" the voice said.

My hand snapped out in front of me. A shadow crossed my face—from the Enforcer walking past, probably. But again I couldn't raise my head to look at him directly. I could only look down, at the shovel he placed in my hand.

What are we digging for? I wanted to ask. *And why? If you can travel between planets and control other people's bodies, surely your technology is advanced enough that you could have* robots *do this work. Wouldn't that work better?*

My body took five steps forward, and I drove the shovel into the ground, as deep as I could. I brought up a shovelful of dirt that included three pea-shaped pebbles that were an odd, mottled grayish blue. I stood there with the shovel aloft, and Rosi's hands reached into the dirt and pulled out the pebbles. She dropped them into a bucket that materialized beside us. Once she'd wiped away the top layer of dirt, she found four more pebbles. This continued until my shovel was empty. Then she stood back, and I brought up a second shovelful of dirt.

Beside me, Enu and Edwy were following the same process, at the exact same pace.

Oh, I thought. *Oh no*.

The Enforcers didn't need robots to mine this planet. Because as long as they could control our bodies, *we* were their robots.

CHAPTER FOURTEEN

We worked for hours without a break. Not a real one. We each got a chance to go to the bathroom, but even that was automated: We'd finish a hole, and three of us were forced to go on to the next section, while one of us stayed behind to pee.

So . . . is the urine important to whatever we're mining here? I wondered. *Are we mining, or are we growing and harvesting some sort of living minerals?*

Was there such a thing in the universe as a living mineral?

My hand ached with the desire to reach back into my pocket for my phone, to check out everything I could find about other planets. Our schools back in Refuge City hadn't included much information about the rest of the universe, and I'd always had my own reasons for avoiding the topic. So I *needed* the Internet.

I couldn't get my hand to do anything but twitch. And,

anyhow, I already knew that my phone couldn't connect.

If only I'd fiddled more with it last night, to see if I could adapt it to the local system. If only I'd held on to the Enforcer communication device, back on Earth, and brought that with me. . . .

While my brain got stuck on regrets and if-onlys, my hands propelled the shovel into the dirt, again and again.

The sun climbed higher and higher into the sky, then began to sag down toward the horizon again. Periodically Rosi and I switched off chores: I dug and she hunted for pebbles; then she dug and I hunted for pebbles. I got blisters on my hands from the shovel; the blisters rubbed raw and broke and bled. The open sores got filthy from the hours of pebble hunting.

That's how wounds get infected! I wanted to scream at the Enforcer. *Even if you don't care about me as a person, don't you care if your robots all get gangrene and our hands rot off?*

By midafternoon, my hands hurt so bad I wanted to sob. But even this was out of my control. My tear ducts stayed dry. My face stayed smooth and untroubled. My mouth stayed silent. I kept digging.

I will go insane if I can't do something, I told myself.

I remembered how I'd gotten my hand to twitch, trying to reach for my phone; how I'd gotten my fingers to sway ever so slightly when I wanted to wipe my face.

Try moving parts of your body that don't have anything to do with shoveling. Or with staying silent.

It took maybe an hour of trying, but I managed to wiggle my right ear a millimeter up, and then another millimeter down.

Oh, and that's so useful! I thought scornfully. *One wiggling ear—that's going to help me signal for help! That's going to enable me to escape and rescue the others!*

I passed another hour too demoralized and too much in pain to do anything but bend forward, dig the shovel into the dirt, lift the shovel, wait for Rosi to search for pebbles, and then do it all over again.

Then some of the dirt dribbled onto my sandals.

Look at me now, you stupid Enforcer! I wanted to scream. *I could be buried in dirt, and you wouldn't even notice! I can't do anything about it! What if the dirt trips me and I fall over—and then Enu digs a shovel into me, because he can't stop himself?*

It was a horrible image. I wanted to scream and cry and rage, but of course I could do nothing but keep digging.

What if I just tried to wiggle my toes? What if I could clear away the dirt that way?

I needed my toes for balance, each time I drove the shovel into the ground. But when I was just standing and waiting for Rosi to sort through the dirt, it didn't matter so much if my toes were clenched or relaxed.

I managed to twitch the little toe on my right foot, sending a tiny clump of dirt off the side of my sandal.

Victory! I told myself.

Or, at least, an infinitesimally small step in the right direction.

I had to look down the next time I dug the shovel into the ground, and what I saw then made me want to gasp.

It wasn't that I'd cleared away that much dirt. I could barely even tell the difference between the level of dirt beside the little toe and the amount beside the toe next to it. What stunned me was what was left behind:

One of the pea-size pebbles lay between my toes.

Oh, hold on to it! I told myself. *Keep it, and then tonight . . . tonight you can figure everything out!*

Maybe it was a crystal that could be used to build some sort of communication device. Or . . .

Oh, right. There's no Internet to tell me how to build something like that. No Internet to help me analyze it.

My heart sank, but I did my best to press my toes together the rest of the afternoon. I did my best to think through anything I'd ever learned about precious minerals.

They wouldn't have us mining all these pea-shaped pebbles for nothing, would they?

CHAPTER FIFTEEN

The sun was setting the last time I stabbed the shovel into the ground—and this time, rather than immediately lift it up again, my hands let go. I stepped away from the shovel and Rosi straightened up before me, and both of us marched toward the concrete doorway alongside Edwy and Enu.

I wanted to scream at the others, *We're done! They're finally letting us stop!* But my mouth still wouldn't move; my throat wouldn't release so much as a peep. I couldn't even look directly at any of them to see if they were as filthy as I was, to see if they were as blistered and bloodied and sore. All I could do was try to clench my toes tightly together, to hold on to the one pebble I'd managed to keep there the entire afternoon.

As soon as I stepped through the concrete doorway, I was hit with a blast of water. First, it just struck my mouth, and I swallowed and swallowed and swallowed, gratefully. Then a sudsier spray covered me from head to toe. The force of the water jerked my head back; it seemed strong enough to scour the skin off my face and arms and hands.

I was glad that my phone—still in my back pocket—was waterproof and buttoned in. But no matter how hard I tried to keep my toes pressed tightly together, I could feel them splaying outward, just as my fingers spread wide to be cleaned thoroughly. The water zapped away all the dirt.

But not the pebble! Try to hold on to the pebble! my brain screamed.

Finally the blast of water stopped, and my dripping body began descending the stairs. A blast of hot air hit me, drying me and my clothes instantly.

My right foot shifted in its sandal. Was there the tiniest lump under the ball of my foot? Could it be that all that water and hot air had only driven the pebble into a better hiding place?

It drove me crazy that I couldn't bend down and check. My feet kept climbing down. My whole body ached so badly from the day of hard labor that I wondered how my legs didn't just crumple beneath me.

We reached the bottom of the stairs again, and once again we were in total darkness. Just as we had the night before, we all turned left, and once again I heard the clang of a gate or a prison door slamming shut behind us.

That means they're going to let you have control of your body again. Right . . . Right . . .

No matter how I tried to lock my knees, I still fell. Once again I landed on Enu, but I quickly rolled away and reached for my foot.

"I'm going to kill that Enforcer! I will!" Enu raged in the darkness. "Nobody treats me like that and gets away with it!"

"At least Bobo and Cana and Zeba didn't have to do that," Rosi said. "All day long, that's what I kept telling myself, to be grateful that they're safe and far away from here. . . ."

I could hear the tears in her voice.

Edwy sniffed.

"We need a plan," he said.

"Shh," I said. "I have the start of one."

"What is it?"

"Tell us!"

"Did you figure out how to get out of here?"

Their questions came so thick and fast, I couldn't even tell who asked what. All I had was a pebble. Maybe I shouldn't get the others' hopes up.

"Maybe the Enforcers are listening," I said. "I'll show you when I can. But did any of you notice anything useful while we were working?"

"Are you kidding?" Enu snarled. "They wouldn't let me turn my head to look at anything but rocks and dirt!"

While he talked, I pulled the pebble from my sandal. I kept both hands over top of it, just in case the Enforcer was watching us with some sort of night-vision goggles.

"Did anybody else notice the other work groups?" Rosi asked softly.

"What?" Edwy and I said together. I was so stunned I almost dropped the pebble.

"I could only see them out of the corner of my eye," Rosi admitted. "Maybe a kilometer away. Eight people? Ten? I think they were all adults."

"What if this whole planet is full of prisoners?" Edwy asked.

"We could join together and rebel," Enu said.

"Sure we could. If the Enforcers didn't control us every minute of the day," I said, then instantly wished I hadn't.

The other three fell silent.

"What are the pebbles for?" Edwy asked. "How many Enforcers are guarding us? Where do they go during the day while we're working?"

"Why don't you ask some important questions?" Enu asked. "Like when are they going to feed us next?"

I felt around the entire surface of the pebble. It was round and smooth—it might as well have been a smaller version of the glass marbles my father talked about playing with as a child. Still keeping it sheltered with my left hand, I tried to dig my right thumbnail into the center of it.

My thumbnail broke.

Automatically, I reached for my phone. I could take a picture of the pebble and ask the Internet to identify it for me, and then . . .

No connection, remember?

I pulled my phone from my back pocket anyhow. At least I could shine the light from the phone's screen onto the pebble, still keeping it under the cover of my hand. At least I could use the phone *somehow.*

I tapped the phone to turn it back on. Nothing happened. I tapped again. Still nothing. Nothing, nothing, nothing . . .

"It won't work!" I gasped. "My phone won't work!"

"So? It didn't work last night, either," Enu said almost accusingly.

"No, this is worse! It won't even turn on! It's dead! I'll never be able to do anything with it! How can this be happening?"

I couldn't get enough air into my lungs. I'd believed, all day long, that I *would* be able to get my phone to work again, that I would be able to use it somehow to save us all from this horrible place, that my brilliance with technology would get us all out of here.

But I couldn't even use the flashlight app. My phone was worthless. My brilliance was worthless. Being able to think didn't even matter.

My life might as well be over right now.

I realized I was wailing.

"Kiandra, calm down," Rosi begged. "Maybe . . . just tell us what you were planning to do. We'll help. I'm sure we can all work together to figure this out, without the phone."

Her voice trembled. She wasn't sure. She wasn't any more certain of anything than I was.

I stopped caring that the Enforcers might overhear us. Because there wasn't any hope anyway.

"It doesn't matter!" I snarled at Rosi. "None of us can do anything! I smuggled one of the pebbles down here with my foot, but—"

"Well, that's kind of cool," Edwy said admiringly. "I didn't even think of trying that. How did you do it?"

"Don't you get it? I worked so hard to hold on to the pebble with my toes, and so what?" I screamed. "That didn't do any good. I don't even know what it is. I can't even *look* at it! And it's not like we can throw a lot of pebbles at the Enforcer who watches us, and kill him like Enu wants, because, duh, the pebble's too small, and anyhow, during the day we can't do anything the Enforcer doesn't want us to do—"

"Except you managed to pick up a pebble," Rosi said quietly. "And hide it until we got down here."

"But that doesn't matter!" I screamed, throwing all my fury and fear into yelling at Rosi.

"Let me see that pebble," Enu said.

I felt his hand on my arm, jerking my hand toward him.

I felt the pebble slip between my fingers.

I heard it hit the floor.

"Now look what you've done!" I yelled at Enu. "You made me drop it!"

"We can find it again," Rosi said, like she was talking to a little child. Her brother, maybe. "We'll all look."

I began sliding my hand across the floor. I needed to get a grip. No matter how annoying she sounded, Rosi was actually right. Maybe the pebble was right where I heard it land. Or no, maybe it had bounced or rolled a little . . .

Something snagged in a small crack under my little finger. Was it just loose mortar? I pressed down hard, bringing my fingers together. It was the pebble under my fingertips! But I felt it give way, like chalk on concrete.

"It's breaking!" I shrieked. "It's broken!"

I heard a sound like the striking of a match.

And suddenly there was light everywhere.

CHAPTER SIXTEEN

I scrambled back, my brain shooting isolated words at me: *Explosion! Danger! Watch out!*

But nothing exploded. Nothing changed—nothing *had* changed—except that we were all bathed in warm, glowing light. I could see the furrows in Enu's forehead, the eyelashes surrounding Edwy's widened eyes, the chipped fingernails on the hand Rosi clapped over her mouth.

I slapped my hand back over the pebble, and instantly we were plunged into darkness again.

"When the guard comes, let me do the talking," I told the others, hoping they understood: *We'll make him think we don't know anything about the pebble. We'll make him think it stayed on our clothes by mistake, and it's gone now, and . . .*

And how would I hide it if he insisted on searching us and our cell?

"What *was* that?" Edwy asked.

"Shh!" I hissed.

My heart thumped so hard against my chest. I waited.

Nothing happened.

"Kiandra, I don't think the guard *is* coming," Rosi whispered. "I don't think he's watching or listening to us now."

"We're already in a cage. Why would he bother watching us?" Enu asked.

My heartbeat slowed down ever so slightly.

"Can you *please* let us see again?" Edwy asked. "Before the light burns out and we've wasted it all?"

Oh, no—what if I've already wasted it all?

I pulled my hand back, and we were lucky: The light glowed out from the pebble once again, clear and beautiful. Rosi grinned. Edwy raised his eyebrows. Enu blinked in astonishment. I could see them all perfectly well.

I could also see the hard gray walls that surrounded us on three sides—stone, maybe? Something synthetic that was even stronger than stone? The floor and ceiling seemed to be made of the same substance as the walls, and any hopes I might have had of tunneling out died instantly.

The fourth side of our prison cell was lined with thick bars that could have been iron or steel or whatever counted as this planet's strongest metal. Even if we'd had the right tools, I don't think we could have sawed through those bars.

Then I saw that some of the bars were already missing.

"Quick! That way! Let's get out of here while we can!

While the light still works!" I pointed at the section of our cage that was completely open. Beyond it was a blank wall—and the hallway we'd walked down before.

Enu, with his athlete's instincts, sprang up immediately and sprinted toward the gap in the bars. He leaped out of the cell like a runner crossing the finish line. He raised his arms in the air, victorious.

Edwy, Rosi, and I were a little slower. The other two paused to glance around cautiously. I waited to scoop up the pebble, to carry it with us. And just in the few moments we'd been crouched in the prison cell, my muscles had gone stiff from the long day of work. It hurt to step forward.

But by the time we reached the gap in the bars, it was gone. The bars from the other side of the cage slid silently in front of us, blocking our way.

"So that's how this works," Edwy said. "They were lazy. They didn't think they had to build a whole cage because they didn't think we'd ever have enough light to see it."

"And they didn't think anyone would run as fast as Enu," Rosi agreed.

"Well, nobody would, in the dark," Edwy said.

"We have to split up," I said.

I jogged over to the other side of the prison cell, and the bars followed me. Quickly, Edwy and Rosi stepped out of the cage, joining Enu out in the hall.

"Now you just have to run as fast as me," Enu told me.

His eyes shone like they always did when he'd been playing basketball. It was like he'd forgotten that we were on another planet, forgotten that the Enforcers had taken over Earth and could take over our bodies. For him this was just another sport.

I'm not good at sports like you are! I wanted to snarl at him.

But I nodded and clutched the glowing pebble in my hand and dashed toward Enu, Edwy, and Rosi.

The bars slid ahead of me, and I slammed into them so hard my head bounced back.

"Try again," Edwy said.

"You can do it!" Rosi encouraged.

I swerved back to the left and aimed for an escape out into the other end of the hall.

Once again I slammed into bars.

"It's like the prison bars are playing keep-away with you," Enu said. "Remember playing that when we were little? Remember how to win?"

I remembered watching *Enu* play keep-away. I didn't remember ever playing it myself.

I certainly didn't remember ever winning that game. And now my forehead throbbed where I'd hit the bars. My legs ached. My ears started ringing so badly that I couldn't hear Enu's advice.

I'm the one who found the pebble, I thought. *But all I did was help the others escape and now I'm left behind. I'll be a prisoner forever.*

I couldn't breathe. I swayed back and forth, and the bars blurred before me. The gravity, which I thought I'd adjusted to, seemed to be pulling me down, harder and harder.

"Enu," I heard Edwy say sharply. "You go back in there and let her out. Then *you* try winning at keep-away."

Suddenly I wished the light coming from the pebble in my hand weren't so bright and steady. Because I could see Enu's face too clearly. I could see the way his eyes hardened.

He didn't want to help me. He didn't want to be the one stuck in the prison cell, the one left behind and trapped while everyone else had a chance at freedom.

He was just as scared as I was.

Edwy shoved Enu's shoulder.

"I'm going! I'm going!" Enu said, jumping back into the prison cell. The bars didn't move at all, probably because he was going in, not out. "Don't worry—I'm fast. I've got this!"

He feinted toward the bars, trying for escape this time. His motion made the bars slide back toward him, and let me step out into the hallway.

I was out of the cage.

"Thank you," I whispered.

I wasn't sure that Enu heard. He was concentrating too

hard. He dashed right, then left, then right again, as if faking out the swiftly sliding bars. Maybe they were designed to speed up when challenged, because they seemed to be going faster and faster.

Finally Enu walked slowly back to the other side of the prison cell, like he was giving up. He sank to the floor. He waited a moment.

And then, with a burst of speed, he sprang to his feet, sped toward the gap in the bars, and dived through it. He rolled into a somersault and landed at my feet.

"All right!" Edwy congratulated him with a high five as Enu stood up.

"That was amazing!" Rosi agreed.

"Not bad," I said, because that's how Enu and I always treated each other. He didn't need to know how close I'd been to panic.

Enu held his arms aloft again, pumping them up and down like he was cheering for himself.

"I knew I could do it," Enu said. "No sweat."

But he actually did have sweat dripping down his T-shirt.

"Why don't you already have your sandal off, to use it to unlock that door at the top of the stairs?" he asked me, pointing down the hall, toward the stairway we'd descended after our long day of work. "Let's *really* get out of here!"

"Let's think about this first," I said. "Make a plan.

Remember, the Enforcer said it gets really cold outside overnight. Rosi's the only one who's wearing more than shorts and a T-shirt, and even her dress looks pretty lightweight. Maybe we can find some other clothes first. And even if they aren't monitoring what we do in our prison cell, doesn't it seem like—"

"If you had your way, you'd sit around thinking your whole life away," Enu interrupted. He gave a disgusted snort. "Come on—let's get out of here. Now!"

Without waiting for an answer, he took off for the stairs.

"Hey! I'm coming too!" Edwy called, darting off after Enu.

"But—" Rosi reached for Edwy's arm, but he slipped away.

"Boys," I grunted. "They think we're going to rescue them when they get in trouble."

I made my voice sound cavalier—casual, even—as though I didn't really care. As though nothing was at stake. But tension churned in my stomach. Tears glistened in Rosi's eyes.

"If we can't get out of here, we can't get back to Earth and Refuge City to find Bobo and Cana and Zeba," she whispered. "We *can't* fail at this."

"Let's go talk some sense into Enu, then," I said, grabbing Rosi's hand and tugging her along. "Sense *and* caution."

I didn't actually know what made sense. What if this was our only chance to escape? What if the guard caught Enu at the door and beat him up or . . . did something even worse? What if . . .

Rosi and I had just reached the bottom of the stairs when we saw Enu coming back toward us. Enu climbed robotically back down the stairs, planting each foot precisely. He kept his elbows bent at exact ninety-degree angles, and pumped his arm in sync with his legs, like he was marching. His head stayed erect, his eyes pointed directly forward, even though it would have made more sense to look down at his feet.

He looked like a robot again, like the Enforcers had him entirely under their control.

I had seen this before, of course, when my body had been under the Enforcers' control too. But the Enforcers had controlled what I saw then, so I'd only gotten isolated glimpses of Enu and the others. I couldn't gape.

This was so much more horrifying, to be able to follow every move of Enu the Automaton. Enu usually moved like liquid, flowing wherever he wanted to go. His every action had always been such a combination of athletic grace and laziness. So it was beyond wrong to see him move with militaristic precision.

It was like watching a stranger. A stranger who just happened to have my brother's face.

A stranger without a soul.

Edwy was balanced on the stairs directly below Enu, and Enu almost knocked him over going past. Edwy barely managed to press his body against the wall, to keep from falling.

Enu reached the bottom of the steps, and Rosi and I did the same thing as Edwy, automatically moving back against the wall in horror, in shame, in numbness. We were in a panic to get out of the way. Was it just our own brains telling us this, or were the Enforcers controlling us in some minor way as well? It was hard to tell.

Enu stepped back into our prison cell, marched to the center of it, and then fell to the floor. He hit hard, his face slamming against stone. It was like watching someone drop a puppet, someone who didn't care if the puppet broke or not.

I couldn't help myself. I ran to my brother's side.

"Are you all right?" I cried, grabbing him by the shoulders. "Did they hurt you?"

"I'm fine," Enu growled, shoving my hands away.

I couldn't tell if he was lying or not. He already had a welt rising on his cheek, but at least the skin wasn't broken.

"How—? Why—?" Edwy sputtered behind me.

"Don't you see?" I said bitterly. "They probably don't even have to lock that door at the top of this stairs. And this is why they don't need complete bars on our prison cell."

"Because *that's* how they keep us from escaping," Rosi

said, pointing at Enu. Her hand shook. The bleakness in her voice echoed off the walls. "They take over our bodies any time we try."

"But not our brains," I said fiercely. "We still have control of our brains."

My words sounded like Enu's glib *I'm fine*.

Really, we had nothing left but bravado.

CHAPTER SEVENTEEN

Enu being Enu, he had to try three more times to mount the stairs and grab the doorknob. Each time, just as he reached the landing at the top of the stairs, his body turned around and started climbing down. Watching from the bottom of the stairs, Edwy, Rosi, and I could see the exact moment he lost control: His entire body went stiff. His movements instantly became jerky.

It didn't scare me any less to see this happen again and again.

"Next time," Enu said stubbornly, the fourth time his invisible puppet master slammed him back to the floor in our cell.

"Enu—every single time you do that, they drop you to the floor harder. What happens when you break a bone?" I asked.

"My bones are too strong for that," he bragged. He lifted his right arm and flexed the muscle. As if that mattered. Then he rolled to the side, clearly preparing to race the bars and escape the cell yet again. "This is like basketball conditioning.

No pain, no gain. Anyhow, what do you want me to do instead? Sit here and do nothing? Just wait for that light to go out?"

I looked down at the pebble I still held in the palm of my hand. The light glowed out evenly and unchanged, filling the space around us.

"I'm *not* doing nothing," I said. "I've been thinking—"

"Nothing *worthwhile*," Enu sneered.

I saw how it could get ugly between us. Enu and I, we were really good at arguing. Something inside me *wanted* to argue—to blame Enu for everything.

We wouldn't even be on this planet if Enu hadn't broken that TV back in Refuge City and made me feel like we had to go out into the store. No, let's go farther back—if he hadn't made me so mad I sided with Edwy and agreed to help him rescue Rosi and confront the Enforcers . . . or if . . .

It would feel so good to scream accusations at Enu. It would feel good to call him names: *Knucklehead! Lamebrain! Sexist!* It would even feel good to punch him.

"Calm down, you two," Rosi said softly. "We're all upset. Why don't we look for a different exit?"

I realized I'd already balled up my fists. I'd already taken a threatening step toward Enu.

Even though he was crumpled on the floor, with bruises swelling on both sides of his face.

"What do you mean, a different exit?" I asked Rosi. My

voice came out just as surly as it did when I snarled at Enu. "Do you see any other door?"

"No, but maybe if we go that way, we will," Rosi suggested. She pointed away from the stairs.

"You mean, *deeper* into the prison?" Enu asked, as if suddenly he and I were on the same side. "That's crazy!"

This was a mild insult, coming from Enu, but Rosi flinched.

Oh, yeah—those Fredtown kids were so pampered and babied. Rosi probably can't cope with any insult.

"It's worth a try," Edwy said, and somehow he sounded calm and patient. "Better than letting them beat you up all night long."

"Or maybe we just need to throw off the Enforcers' system by having *two* of us try to escape at once," Enu said. "Maybe it works like the prison bars. You guys are depending on me too much. I can't be the only brave one! Edwy, help me out here!"

It bugged me that Enu was asking Edwy to be his assistant, and not me.

"What, you think only a *boy* would be capable of helping?" I asked.

"I thought you were too busy *thinking*," Enu taunted. "Besides, Edwy's a faster runner."

"He is not!" I said. "Here, *I'll* help. Race you to the top of the stairs!"

I took off ahead of Enu, knowing he'd catch up quickly. Which he did a split second later, digging his elbow into my rib, shoving me to the side. We mounted the narrow stairs together.

"You jump, I'll dive," he muttered, and I knew he meant at the top of the stairs. He was thinking we could force the door open by slamming into it full strength. He thought one of us was sure to get through.

Oh, Enu, you optimist, you, I thought.

I am not a runner—computer geek, remember? So even though Enu seemed to be trying to stay right beside me, he reached the landing a little ahead of me. I saw him spin around an instant before my own body stiffened and whipped out of my control. My feet stopped climbing up and methodically stepped down instead.

No different from before, I told myself. *Stay calm. As soon as you get back to the prison cell, you'll have control back.*

But I couldn't stay calm. Something *was* different from before. It wasn't just that my body moved without my control; it felt like my mind had been invaded too. Or maybe my spirit—whatever part of me registered joy or sorrow, determination or the desire to give up. As my feet descended the stairs—down and down and down—sad images flooded my mind: a cruel nanny beating Enu and me when we were little; me staring at a computer screen detailing the massacres in my parents' hometown, the first time I'd learned what had really happened there; the Enforcers marching into Refuge City only yesterday, in another lifetime and on another planet. The terror and fear I'd felt fleeing the Enforcers back in Refuge City multiplied and magnified with every step I took. I felt such despair that if I'd had any control over my body, I would have begun weeping and wailing; I would have begun bashing my head against the wall.

Maybe I would have even hurled myself down the stairs.

Just a few more steps and you'll be at the bottom anyhow, I tried to tell myself. *Just another dozen or so steps after that, and you'll be back in the cell. You'll be yourself again.*

It was still agony, every step my body took against my will. It was even worse agony because I couldn't cry, I couldn't wail—I couldn't even shift the straps of my sandals where they rubbed on my blistered feet.

And then Enu and I were back in the prison cell, landing in a jumbled heap together.

The tears I hadn't been able to shed before stung my eyes. I kept my face down, hoping I could hide my anguish from Rosi and Edwy, waiting out in the hall.

"Was . . . was it that bad the other four times you ran up there?" I gasped to Enu. "Did walking down make you feel sad every single time?"

Maybe he was surprised I brought it up. Maybe he was still caught in the sorrow that the Enforcers had slammed into us. But for once, Enu answered a simple question with naked honesty.

"Yes," he murmured, blinking back tears of his own. (Tears! Enu never cried!) "It's gotten worse with every try."

Worse? Was it possible to feel any worse?

And Enu had known that it got worse every time, and he still kept trying?

I stared into my brother's eyes, and he stared back at me. Our eyes matched, I knew, both a glowing green.

"You," I said, "are either the bravest idiot, or the most idiotic brave person who's ever lived."

"Am I supposed to say thank you?" he asked.

He attempted a mocking grin, which failed dramatically. I gave him a weak punch in the arm because I had to do that—we had to be ourselves again.

"*Now* are you two ready to go looking for another door?" Edwy called from out in the hall.

Even though my legs still trembled, I forced myself to stand up. Even though my voice wavered, I forced myself to call back, "Yes. Absolutely."

I tried to shake off the lingering sorrow and hopelessness. *I'm not letting the Enforcers control what I think and feel,* I told myself. *Not ever again. Not if I can help it.*

The question was, could I help it?

Did I have any control over *that*?

CHAPTER EIGHTEEN

For our first several steps headed away from the stairs and our prison cell, the hallway ahead of us looked no different from the hallway behind us. Empty cells lay to our left and right, and dirty footprints showed that many others had walked here before us.

Are these human footprints or Enforcer footprints? I wondered.

There were so many of them, and so layered on top of one another, that it was impossible to tell.

Not that I would be able to tell the difference between the footprints anyhow. Not without my phone camera, and access to the Internet to compare images, and . . .

"How many prisoners do you think there are?" Edwy asked. "How many prisoners used to live here? Or—are there some who are still out working? Do they have prisoners working in shifts?"

"If there were enough to fill all these cages, we would have seen them," Rosi said. "Maybe the Enforcers set them free? And sent them home? And they'll set us free again soon too?"

Her optimistic tone sounded totally wrong in this grim place. It seemed totally wrong while I was still fighting the despair from my forced march down the steps.

Edwy and Rosi kept peering around, looking at everything. I was doing well to put one foot in front of the other. I managed to glance back to see if Enu was similarly affected: He trudged along just as doggedly, his head down, his shoulders slumped.

He did run into that agonizing despair five times. Knowingly, the last four times.

I guessed he had learned something about persistence, playing basketball all the time. I guessed maybe he was braver than I thought.

"Doesn't that light seem really strange?" Edwy asked, glancing over his shoulder at me.

"Yeah, because it's a pebble that lights up a whole prison," Enu snarled. "That *is* strange. We're on another planet. We're in a *prison*. Everything's strange here!"

"No, I mean, think about how a flashlight works," Edwy said. "It spreads out, and so it's harder and harder to see, the farther out you look."

"With a laser, the glow doesn't spread out," Rosi pointed out. "That's a type of light too."

"But that's a narrow beam, and a laser light goes on and on and on, unless it runs into something," Edwy said. "This pebble light . . . the glow is the same all around us, just as strong out at the edges as it is right beside us. And it keeps changing how far ahead of us it goes."

Because I'm holding the pebble, and I keep walking forward, I wanted to growl at him. *How stupid are you?*

But then I saw what he meant. The light flowed out evenly up to the very end of a prison cell six spaces ahead of us. And then, when I took another step forward, the light didn't move up an equal amount, one step's worth. Instead it leaped far enough ahead to reach the end of the next cell— the equivalent of maybe eight steps farther.

It was like the light had a mind of its own, like the pebble was thinking about how much it wanted to show us.

Can we trust it? I wondered, oddly.

But when you've barely escaped a dark prison cell and you have only one light—and when you've just been purposely plunged into despair and hopelessness—that light is going to be unbearably precious, whether you trust it or not.

I cradled the pebble even more carefully in my cupped hands.

"I wish we had the Internet to look up how it works," I said wistfully.

"Do you think there was any information about this

planet or its pebbles on the Internet we had back on Earth?" Edwy asked. "Or the Internet that Rosi and I had back in Fredtown?"

"The Freds wouldn't have wanted us to know about any place where children were kept in a prison like this," Rosi said, so softly that the words came out almost as a whimper. "Without even a trial, without getting to say good-bye to their family and friends . . ."

I could tell she was thinking about Bobo, Cana, and Zeba again.

"Do you think the Freds even *know* about this planet?" Edwy asked. "Or this prison? Do people back on Earth know?" He turned to me. "Do you remember seeing anything about Enforcer prison planets online before . . . well, before we were on one?"

"No, but, Edwy, I couldn't have ever seen everything that was on the Internet," I protested. "There was too much information for that. Even in an entire lifetime . . ."

"But you knew all about the Freds," he said stubbornly.

Because I hated them, I wanted to tell him. *I read about them when I wanted to feel bitter and depressed. Because I always thought they'd ruined my life by not taking me to a Fredtown too.*

"I never thought any other aliens besides Freds would ever come to Earth," I admitted. "And . . . nobody ever wanted to talk about the other species out in the universe. It was too painful. Too much of a reminder, maybe, that humans are so much weaker, by comparison."

Did he know how almost all the discussion of alien life had taken place in secret, out of the public eye? Did he know how people had talked, before he and Rosi and the other kids from the Fredtowns all came back? People had whispered constantly, *How do we even know that those Freds aren't keeping our children as slaves? How do we know that they're not doing terrible things to our babies? How do we know that they aren't bashing them in the heads as newborns . . . and all our children are dead?*

I'd seen the horrible websites with their hateful rumors, their doctored pictures, their blatant lies. If I'd lived with parents who'd loved and protected me—or even nannies who'd cared—I never would have been allowed to see such things.

Of course Edwy didn't know any of that. Pretty much everything he'd learned about Earth and Earth's people—and reality—he'd learned from Enu and me.

"Why are we talking about any of this?" Enu asked grumpily. "Who cares how some stupid light works, when we're trapped in a prison? Who cares about what was or wasn't online, when *we're* never going to see any of it again? When there's not another door anywhere, and this hallway has nothing but one empty cage after another. . . ."

Maybe he was still carrying around the despair from the stairs.

"*Are* they all empty?" Edwy asked. "What about that one?"

He pointed toward a prison cell at the far end of the light's reach. I saw a flash of mossy green and brown on the floor of that cell, as if someone had left a blanket or a towel behind. Or just a rag. But something about that barely visible scrap seemed familiar, as if I ought to recognize it. As if I *would* recognize it, if it weren't so out of place on this alien planet, in this alien prison.

"Is that—?" Rosi suddenly gasped behind me. Then, even though she'd been raised by ridiculously polite Freds, she elbowed Edwy, Enu, and me out of the way and dashed ahead of us all.

"Cana!" Rosi cried. "Cana! Is that you? Are you all right? Where are Bobo and Zeba?"

CHAPTER NINETEEN

It was indeed Cana.

Enu, Edwy, and I ran after Rosi, all of us calling out questions: "What happened?" "How did you get here?" "How did the Enforcers find you?"

Cana didn't move.

My heart began to beat faster—much faster than it should have, just from running down a hall.

Rosi reached the section of bars surrounding Cana's prison cell, and those bars had the same kind of gap our prison cell had had. Rosi darted inside, crouched down, and scooped Cana into her arms. Edwy and I followed.

Enu stayed outside the prison cell, nervously bouncing back and forth on the balls of his feet.

"Shh," he called, glancing nervously over his shoulder. "Do you have to be so loud? You're going to wake up all the guards! If there are lots of guards . . ."

Cana groggily wrapped her arms around Rosi, then widened the embrace to include Edwy and me.

"This is the best dream . . . ," she murmured. "I knew *someone* nice would find me. . . . What happened before— that was only a nightmare, right?"

What *had* happened to her since we left her in the Emporium of Food storeroom?

Cana kept blinking, her thick eyelashes brushing her round, childish cheeks. She balled her hands into a fist and rubbed her eyes the way a baby or a toddler would.

She had tear tracks on her face.

"Cana, you're awake," Rosi said gently. "This isn't a dream. And however you ended up here alone, it probably felt like a nightmare. But . . . it was real. Is Bobo . . . Did he . . ."

Now that she was face-to-face with Cana, Rosi seemed almost afraid to ask about her brother.

Doesn't she even notice that Cana is wincing at every word Rosi says?

"Don't worry. You're with us now, so everything's okay," I said. My voice came out sounding too hearty. It was like how my parents had talked to Enu and me over the computer when we were little. When I was young and innocent enough to believe their promises and lies.

"Did Zeba and Bobo come here with you?" Edwy asked.

"They stayed in that food place," Cana said. "They were asleep. I saw everyone else leave, and I just wanted to see . . . And then there was a light. . . . And . . . I ended up here. I'm here. Are you here?"

Cana didn't sound like herself.

How do you know what she sounds like normally? I chided myself. *You didn't even spend a full day with her. And we were running away from Enforcers practically the whole time.*

But even when we ran around like rats in a maze in the basement of the Emporium of Food, Cana was the one to take my hand, which calmed me down. Cana was the one who noticed the **STOREROOM** sign first.

I didn't exactly have a lot of experience hanging out with five-year-olds, but she'd seemed old for her age; she'd seemed a *lot* older and more mature than Bobo.

Now she sounded like she was younger than five.

How long had she been alone? Had she started to wonder if she would ever see any of her friends again?

In my mind I could see Enu and me when we were little. The image was as grim as what the Enforcers had shown me on the stairs, but *I* was the one calling up this memory. One of the places we'd lived had had dark shadows that crawled across the walls every night; that was one of the periods when we'd had a particularly mean nanny. It was hard to remember now, but back then Enu and I had fallen asleep every night holding hands. We'd whispered to each other, *Don't look! Keep your eyes shut! There's nothing there! Really, there isn't!*

We truly had watched out for each other, back then. But

what if I hadn't had Enu? What if I'd faced those shadows and that mean nanny alone?

Even with Enu around, I'd cried a lot back then.

Maybe that had all happened when I was five.

I lifted Cana from the floor, pulling her away from Rosi and Edwy.

"We'll get you out of here," I promised.

"Good luck with that," Enu said sarcastically.

I turned: While the rest of us had run into Cana's prison cell, he'd run past it, and past the next two empty cells too. I hadn't noticed, because I'd been so focused on Cana, but Enu had found another door. This one was right in the middle of the hallway, not at the top of any stairs. So it was doubtful that it led up to the planet's surface. Still, Enu was tugging on the door handle. Then he kicked it and beat his fists against the smooth surface. His muscles bulged and the veins in his neck stood out with the exertion.

The door didn't budge.

"Weren't you just telling *us* to be quiet?" I asked him. Still holding on to Cana, I stepped toward the gap in the bars of her cage. Instantly the gap slid closed before me, and Cana let out a whimper.

"I'll help you get out," Edwy said. "Then you can pick the lock for Enu."

He moved toward the new gap that had opened up. The bars slid toward him, and that let me step out.

"It's not going to do any good," Enu grumbled. "Nobody could pick this lock. There *isn't* a lock."

"*I* can take care of it," I said with confidence I didn't actually feel.

But when I stepped up to the door, I saw that he was right. The doorknob was smooth and solid and seemingly all one piece with the door. I couldn't even see how it might turn, let alone how to pick it.

I felt like the walls were closing in on me.

"We are completely and utterly trapped," Enu said, and the hopelessness in his voice was as thick and overwhelming as anything I'd felt on the stairs, under the Enforcers' control. "There's no way out."

CHAPTER TWENTY

We might have stood there all night, staring hopelessly at an unmovable door, if Cana hadn't started crying again. This roused Rosi and Edwy, who huddled around her and began patting her arms and head and murmuring, "There, there. It's okay."

"We have to do something," Rosi whispered. "Little children need to know that they are loved. That they'll be protected and kept safe. When . . . when they're going through bad times, they need to know that there are grown-ups they can count on. Or . . ." She glanced back and forth between Edwy, Enu, and me. "At least older kids who know how to take care of them."

I didn't know how to take care of Cana. I didn't know how to take care of anyone. Enu had sweat running down his face in a totally different way from when he came back from playing basketball. I was pretty sure that if I touched his forehead, it would be cold and clammy—like he was so panicked it had made him sick. Edwy was biting his lip so hard it had begun to bleed a little, and his eyes were too large and terrified. Maybe his face had shrunk. He already looked like a smaller version of Enu, so that made it doubly painful to gaze at him. His distraught face made me worry about *both* my brothers.

Even Rosi, who was composed enough to put actual sentences together, looked awful. Her dress was ripped and sagged off one shoulder. Her hair stuck out as if it'd been snagged. Her eyes were just as round and dazed as Edwy's.

"Are you crying because you're scared?" Rosi asked Cana. Her voice was so gentle it made me feel a little comforted. "We won't let anyone hurt you."

"You can't promise that!" Enu protested. "You don't know anything about what's going to happen! When the Enforcers take over our bodies, and we don't have any choice *what* we do, then—"

Rosi shot him a surprisingly firm glare.

"Shut up, Enu," I said.

"Maybe we'll feel better if we just all go to sleep," Edwy said.

"You go to sleep, and everything looks better in the morning," Cana chirped through her tears.

"That's right," Rosi said.

All three of them looked more cheerful already, as if the words they'd spoken had been more than words—a balm, maybe, a salve, a good-luck talisman. This kind of thing had annoyed me back at the Emporium of Food, but here . . .

Maybe I wanted to believe in their good-luck talismans now too.

"No, that's *stupid*," Enu said. "We go to sleep, we wake up, the Enforcers take over our bodies again. We're back to square one."

"But we'll be well rested," Rosi said firmly. "Our brains will work better. And we'll have another day to figure things out. We can search for an exit again tomorrow night, when we're fresher."

"When our pebble light probably won't work anymore," Enu scoffed. "Or the Enforcers have taken it away from us. Or . . ." I could practically see Enu's brain working, trying to come up more reasons to mock Rosi.

"Rosi and Cana and I are going to sleep," Edwy said, and even though his voice squeaked a little, he sounded more grown-up than Enu. "You and Kiandra can do whatever you want."

If I'd said something like that, it would have come out like a taunt, and it would have been clear that I was really saying, *I think you're making a stupid choice, but whatever! Go ahead and ruin your life—I don't care!* But Edwy made his words sound like . . . kindness. Acknowledging that we all had free choice.

"We only have one light," Enu said.

"We don't need a light to sleep," Rosi said.

She lifted Cana from my arms, and it was weird how bereft that made me feel—as if I was holding on to Cana to comfort myself, even more than I was comforting her.

"Maybe I want to sleep too," I said. I swayed with exhaustion. "Maybe the little kids are right. Maybe it'll help."

Enu narrowed his eyes at me, as if we were supposed to be on the same team and I'd just betrayed him.

"Fine," he practically spat. "Give up. But you should all go back to the same prison cells we were in before, so the Enforcers don't know we figured out how to get out. The four of us should go back to our cage, and that girl"—he pointed at Cana—"should go back to hers."

Cana's chin quivered, as if she was barely holding back sobs. I thought again about Enu and me holding hands in our own childhood, warding off shadows and nightmares together.

"We are not doing that to Cana," I told Enu. "If there are consequences . . . I'll pay them."

I waited for Enu to protest again. This was another promise I couldn't be sure of keeping. It just sounded good. It just felt good.

Apparently, I liked *trying* to be a hero.

Enu kept glaring at me. It felt like anything could happen.

He might beat me up, just to let off steam. He might start screaming and screaming and screaming, letting out the fury and fear the Enforcers had poured into him after his five runs up the stairs.

Or he just might give up.

Enu's shoulders slumped.

"It's not like any of this matters," he said, shrugging. "It's not like we have any control over anything."

Somehow that felt like the worst response he could have chosen.

We went back to our original cage, carrying Cana with us. She was asleep before we'd even taken two steps. I thought I would fall asleep just as rapidly, once we all lay down on the floor of our prison cell and I hid the pebble light so it was totally dark again. I was beyond exhausted; my body had done hard physical labor all day long. But I lay there wide awake for what felt like hours after all the others slipped into the slower breathing of sleep. At first it felt good that we were all huddled together. But then Edwy began to twitch, probably from a nightmare. Rosi moaned and called out plaintively in her sleep: "Bobo! Bobo . . ." Cana's hand on my shoulder and even Enu's forehead pressed against my hair felt like responsibilities, like goading reminders: *You can't blame Enu for breaking that TV back at the Emporium of Food. It's not actually his fault we're here.* You're *the one who led him up the stairs.* You're *the one who had to go find out what was happening, instead of staying safe and secure. . . .* You're *the one who needs to get us all out of here. . . .*

I felt for the pebble in my shorts pocket, where I'd tucked it so the light wouldn't show. That was a responsibility too. We had to keep it hidden from the Enforcers—we had to keep it, period.

But the way I was lying, it could easily roll out. I closed my hand around the pebble, holding it tight. I knew from holding hands with Enu when I was little that I was capable of holding on all night long, even in my sleep.

Apparently my brain was too tired to think clearly. Because in the morning when I woke up, I was still holding on to the pebble—but that wasn't a good thing. No alarm sounded this time; when I opened my eyes, it was because the Enforcers had taken control of my body again. *They* made me open my eyes, even though there was no light around to see with; *they* made me spring up and move robotically toward the feeding trough at the back of the prison cell.

I could still feel the pebble nestled in my clenched hands. Could the Enforcers tell it was there too?

What would they make me do with it?

What would they do to me for having it?

CHAPTER
TWENTY-ONE

My face plunged into the feeding trough, my chin hitting the same slimy gruel I'd eaten the day before. I tried
to remember: Yesterday morning, had the Enforcers made
me lift my hands to hold on to the side of the trough? If they
made me do that today, would I drop the pebble onto the
floor—or into the gruel?

If it landed in the gruel, would the Enforcers make me
eat it?

I almost gagged just thinking about it. But the Enforcers
didn't even let me do that. My face stayed immersed in the
gruel; my mouth kept gobbling it down.

At least my hands *didn't* swing up to hold on to the feeding trough.

*But I will have to open my hand once I'm outside and
holding on to the shovel. If I'm still holding the pebble then,
I'll lose it. I won't have any light to see by down here again,
unless one of us manages to smuggle in another one.*

The thought of losing the pebble and its light made me want to scream. It made me want to throw myself to the floor and flail my arms about in the biggest tantrum ever.

Of course I couldn't force a single sound out of my mouth. I couldn't do anything but keep eating.

I have to find some way to drop the pebble before we're outside, I told myself.

I remembered how I'd managed the day before to move my fingers and toes just a millimeter or two.

Maybe now, I thought. *While the Enforcer just wants me to eat and eat . . . Maybe I can get my fingers . . . to . . .*

Just as I was willing my fingers to open and drop the pebble, I felt a hand on my back.

"Kiandra?" someone whispered.

Did the Enforcers know my name? Had they been watching and eavesdropping all along? What were they going to do to me for stealing the pebble? How would they punish me?

Whoever it was tugged on my hand—my right hand, the one holding the pebble.

The pebble plummeted to the floor, throwing light everywhere.

CHAPTER TWENTY-TWO

It was Cana beside me, grabbing my hand. It was *only* Cana.

My relief died with my second thought.

Are the Enforcers making her be the one to expose me? I wondered in horror. *Are they going to make her do something to hurt me?*

I couldn't even turn my head to look at Cana, so I only caught a glimpse of her out of the corner of my eye. My face stayed pointed stubbornly down, aimed toward the feeding trough, placidly gobbling up gruel. But the light from the pebble flowed all around us—nothing was hidden now.

Somehow Cana managed to tilt her head alongside mine, so she was peering directly at me.

"Kiandra, what are you doing?" Cana asked. She lifted her head slightly, possibly peering at Rosi, Enu, and Edwy on the other side of me. "What's everyone doing? Why won't anyone look at me?" She put her head close to mine again, as if wanting to look me straight in the eye. "Why won't you answer?"

Could it be that she *wasn't* under the Enforcers' control, like all the rest of us?

Because she's not in the right prison cell? Because . . .

I couldn't think of any other reason.

Cana stuck a finger into the gruel in the trough, held it up, looked at it, and tentatively licked her fingertip.

"Yuck!" she said, sticking her tongue out and scraping it back and forth against her teeth, as if trying to get the taste out of her mouth. "My mommy and daddy would *never* make me eat anything like that. Not my Fred-mommy and Fred-daddy, and not my other mommy and daddy either."

She said this matter-of-factly, as if being raised by Fred-parents for five years and then being shifted back to her original parents back in her birthplace had been no big deal. Even if her birthplace was called Cursed Town.

If she can adapt to that, then maybe she'll be okay here, too, I told myself.

Who was I kidding? We were in *prison*. She didn't even understand what was happening, or why nobody would talk to her now.

Not that I understand either . . .

My mouth just kept gobbling gruel. I was almost down to the bare wood of the trough; my tongue began darting out, trying to catch the last drops.

"Do *you* like that food?" Cana asked, wrinkling up her

nose. Then I could almost see her make a conscious effort not to look so disgusted. "Different people like different things, and that's okay. But . . . why won't anybody talk to me? Am I having another dream? Sometimes in dreams people don't act right. My Fred-daddy always said dream people are different, and we can't be mad at real people for how the dream people act. They may look like the same person, but they're not."

Okay, maybe that's the best way for Cana to see things, I thought. *Maybe if she thinks the rest of us are just dream people right now, she won't be scared. Or . . .*

My upper torso jerked up, away from the food trough. Out of the corner of my eye I could see that Rosi, Enu, and Edwy did the same thing, their movements coordinating exactly with mine.

My body pivoted away from the food trough, toward the bars of our prison cell. Everyone but Cana did the same.

"I don't like this dream!" Cana protested. "I want to wake up! I want people to talk to me! I want to go home!"

Cana ran around in front of me, clutching my legs.

"Kiandra, help me!" she begged.

I couldn't even bend my neck to look down at her. Instead, I had to turn my head to watch as first Enu, then Edwy, then Rosi marched forward, toward the hallway and the stairs. This time the bars of the cage slid easily out of the way, letting them through. Probably the same thing had happened yesterday; I just hadn't had any light then to see what was going on.

"Kiandra!" Cana cried again, gripping my knees even tighter.

I could see what was about to happen, but I couldn't stop it. No amount of trying to resist would do any good. I felt my torso lean forward, ever so slightly. My right foot thrust out; my legs ripped themselves out of Cana's grasp.

"Why won't you listen to me?" Cana wailed.

My body marched relentlessly forward, knocking Cana to the floor.

I heard her run after me, but the instant I stepped through the bars, they must have snapped shut behind me. Because all the way up the stairs I could hear Cana crying, "Let me out! Let me out! Come back! Somebody help me!"

And there was nothing I could do.

CHAPTER
TWENTY-THREE

All day long while my body worked—my muscles aching, my blisters multiplying—my mind kept darting around like a nervous ferret: *Is Cana still crying? Did she understand that we weren't leaving her behind on purpose? Why wasn't she forced to come with us? Do the Enforcers even remember that she's there? How are we ever going to get out of this place?*

Dozens of times I tried to reach for the phone in my pocket. I wanted to know what this planet was, what was happening back on Earth, what the pebbles I kept shoveling actually were, what rules allowed the Enforcers to keep us here, how we could get whoever controlled the Enforcers to make them let us go. . . . But I couldn't get my arms and hands to do anything more than twitch—and then keep shoveling and picking through dirt, completely under the Enforcers' control.

And I knew the phone was dead and disconnected anyway.

I shifted to trying to catch another pebble with my toes. What if the first one burned out? What if we'd have to find a pebble every day if we wanted any light at night? Regardless, wouldn't it be good if we had backup?

But my skill the day before must have been beginner's luck. I couldn't dribble any dirt on my sandals. I couldn't edge my little toe off the sandal even to brush a pebble that landed right beside it, let alone grasp the pebble and hold on to it.

I couldn't get my body to do anything I wanted except twitch. And that movement was so small, so slight, that I might have imagined it.

Maybe one of the other kids will go back with a pebble? Maybe Enu or Edwy or Rosi will manage to grab and hold on to something that will help us even more?

I couldn't even catch the other kids' eyes, to signal what they should do.

Finally the daylight dimmed, and I drove the point of the shovel into the ground one last time. We repeated the same routine from the night before: marching back to the stairs, getting hit with the blast of water, getting zapped with the blast of drying heat.

The stairs and the hallway and the prison cell were completely dark again, the descent just as frightening as the two nights before. I hit the floor of the prison cell and immediately began calling, "Cana? Cana? Where are you?"

Rosi called out the same thing. Enu swore, listing all the unspeakable things he wanted to do to the Enforcers. Edwy cried, "Wait, what are you talking about? Wasn't Cana with us the whole day long? I didn't see her, but I just thought the Enforcers weren't letting me. Where is Cana?"

Suddenly there was light everywhere, and Cana was right beside us, dancing around, giggling, and waving the shining pebble over her head.

"Did I surprise you?" she asked, her face stretched into a grin, her green eyes glowing.

Strangely, the grin, the giggle, and the dancing seemed authentic.

"Were you waiting all day to pull that trick on us?" Rosi asked, smiling back. I could see the exhaustion and fear in Rosi's eyes, but maybe Cana couldn't. And how did Rosi keep her voice so gentle?

"Nuh-uh," Cana said, shaking her head emphatically. "When you all left me I cried and cried and cried. Then I remembered my Fred-mommy telling me that crying is okay for a while, but it doesn't solve anything and you have to move on to doing something else. So I went exploring. And I made new friends!"

"Exploring?" Rosi repeated, just as Edwy said, "New friends?"

"She's lying, right?" Enu muttered. "This isn't a place for friends."

I punched him in the arm, our code for *Shut up!* My muscles were so rubbery from the long day of work that the punch carried no force. So I kicked him instead. It wasn't like I exactly believed Cana either, but I wanted to hear what she had to say.

Or maybe I just wanted to know how anyone could act so calm and happy in this prison cell.

"Where did you meet these friends?" I asked. "Did they come here? What did they look like?"

Cana bent her head and peered severely at me.

"You are not supposed to worry about what somebody looks like!" she exclaimed, as if I'd said something shocking. "What really matters about a person is what's inside. Their heart. But . . ." Her eyes darted around and her voice dropped to a whisper. "Is it okay that I noticed that they looked different? Really, really different?"

"Like an Enforcer?" Enu asked. He crossed his arms over his chest. "She thinks she made friends with Enforcers?"

"Shh! Let her tell her own story," I shushed him.

"Alcibiades and Melos and Arkan and all the others are not Enforcers!" Cana exclaimed, as if he'd suggested that up was down, or that the moon was the sun—or that we'd all chosen to be in the horrible prison.

"Show us where they are," I suggested.

"I can't," Cana said, sticking her chin in the air. "They were on the other side of that door beside my cage, and it locks automatically every evening. That's what Alcibiades told me."

"Then jam something in it tomorrow to keep it open," Edwy suggested.

"I can't," Cana said. "Alcibiades says that will just make the Enforcers patrol down here in person until it's fixed."

"Oh, that's convenient," Enu mocked. "So there's no way for *us* to meet your new friends?"

Rosi hovered between Enu and me.

"Sometimes little kids make up imaginary friends to comfort themselves when they're scared," she whispered. "Cana was all by herself, all day long. It must have been terrifying."

"So she *is* just lying," Enu said under his breath.

"It's not exactly lying," Rosi told him. "Lying is bad, but this isn't."

She crouched beside Cana and stroked the little girl's hair.

"Never mind, Cana," she said. "You don't have to show us your new friends. I'm glad you have them with you to keep you company during the day while the rest of us are away."

Edwy knelt beside the two girls and patted Cana's shoulder.

"Get Alcibiades to show you ways to escape," he said. "Get him to show you places to find more food."

I tugged on Enu's arm and took a step back, so we were separated into groups once more: Enu and me on one side of the cage, the three kids raised by Freds on the other.

"They're acting like a five-year-old with an imaginary friend is going to save us?" I snarled at Enu.

It felt good to snarl. It felt like rebellion, like fighting back.

"We're all going to die," Enu said, and then I didn't feel good anymore.

It felt like he was the only one telling the truth.

CHAPTER
TWENTY-FOUR

Cana insisted that "Alcibiades" had explained why she hadn't been forced to go out and work with the rest of us: "It's because I'm too little and young," she said. "He says I have to grow first. Just wait until I'm big and strong like the rest of you!"

You'll never grow big and strong living here, I thought. *We'll have to escape for you to survive at all, and there's no way to do that. . . .*

That made it so I couldn't say anything to Cana. I also couldn't let myself meet Enu's glowering gaze again. I just sat there, like a lump.

But Edwy and Rosi kept chattering away. No matter how much Cana insisted it wouldn't matter, they wanted to test a different theory, the same one I'd thought of before giving up in despair. What if sleeping in a different prison cell was enough to trick the Enforcers' system? What if one of us older kids slept in the wrong cell that night? What would happen then? Would that mean one of us got to stay behind during the day?

Edwy and Rosi discussed this endlessly, long after Cana gave up protesting and fell asleep on the floor. Finally they walked over toward Enu and me.

"Enu, do you think you and I should—" Edwy began, just as Rosi said, "Kiandra, would you like to help me by—"

"Kiandra and I are *not* going to help you with your stupid ideas!" Enu growled at the younger two.

Edwy and Rosi sat in shocked silence for a moment. Then Rosi took Edwy's hand and said, "Come on."

I saw them go to separate cages farther down the hall. They were not just risking the Enforcers' anger; they were also each going to spend the whole night alone.

How could they be so brave? Or stupid?

I felt like I lay awake the entire night, feeling the distance between Enu and me and the younger kids, feeling how badly he and I had failed at protecting everyone back in Refuge City. And there wasn't anything we could do to protect anyone, here on this desolate planet.

And then there are Bobo and Zeba left behind in Refuge City, in danger. And Udans . . .

In the morning when the Enforcers took control of my body, it was worse than ever, because I couldn't look around to see what had happened to Edwy and Rosi. Enu and I ate the awful food in the wooden trough, and I was relieved to see Cana poking hesitantly at it. At least she'd get some nutrition.

Cana held the light up high for Enu and me, and when I spun around I caught a glimpse of Edwy and Rosi standing in the hallway. They both stood so stiffly they might as well have been machines, not humans. Or some minor tool not even as advanced as a machine—they might have been hammers or pliers or wrenches.

So Cana was right, I thought. *Their experiment was useless. It just made everyone fight over nothing.*

The force controlling my body made me step past Cana and out of the prison cell. But it didn't make me line up with Edwy and Rosi. Instead it made me crash into Rosi, knocking her down. Out of the corner of my eye, I saw Enu do the same thing with Edwy. Both of the younger kids dropped without throwing out their arms to catch themselves. Rosi's shoulder slammed into the wall. Edwy fell to his knees.

The Enforcers did that on purpose, I thought. *They're punishing us all.*

And yet I couldn't apologize; I couldn't explain. I had no control at all.

Surely Rosi knows I didn't want to hurt her, I thought. *Surely she understands it was the Enforcer using me.*

Digging was worse than ever that day. It felt like the four of us spent a hundred hours working in the hot sun. Maybe a thousand. But finally the Enforcers marched us back through the doorway, into the harsh spray of water, and down the stairs into our cage. And finally, as soon as we dropped to the floor, I could control my own mouth and sputter out, "I'm sorry, Rosi. I'm so sorry. . . ."

"I know it wasn't your fault," Rosi murmured, even as she rubbed her shoulder.

"You can't do that again," Enu thundered, and I could tell that was his way of apologizing to Edwy, too.

"No, because if we sleep in different cells, they don't feed us," Edwy said, rubbing his stomach ruefully. "At least not me—what about you, Rosi?"

"Nope," Rosi said.

Cana danced up beside us.

"But Alcibiades told me to look in my old prison cell, and look what *I* found!" she crowed. She held out her hand, displaying a small cake of dried grains. "I was saving this for all of us to share tonight, but if Rosi and Edwy didn't get breakfast at all, then . . ."

"Then they should have it all," Enu finished for her.

Maybe I should have been mad that Enu was acting once again like he had all the power to make a decision on behalf of us all. But I was so relieved that Enu wasn't just screaming and snarling. I was so relieved that Rosi and Edwy hadn't been hurt worse. I was so relieved that Cana could stay happy, even trapped in the awful prison.

I looked at Enu over the tops of the younger kids' heads, and mouthed two words: *Thank you.*

CHAPTER
TWENTY-FIVE

Days passed, and they were all the same. We were jerked awake each morning by losing control of our bodies. Then we were forced to eat the nasty slop in the feeding trough, forced to dig pebbles all day from the desolate soil, forced to be sprayed clean, forced to descend the stairs and drop to the floor again in our grubby prison cell. I didn't have a single moment when I wasn't bone-tired, achy-muscled, rubber-limbed, sick, sore, and starving.

I would have said I didn't have a single moment when I wasn't full of despair, but . . . somehow there was a golden moment I looked forward to every day: the moment Enu, Edwy, Rosi, and I got back to our cell, regained control of ourselves, shared the small, crumbly food that Cana brought us from her former prison cell, and heard Cana's gleeful retelling of *her* day with Alcibiades and her other friends.

"Alcibiades says if you hold your breath while you eat, the food doesn't taste so bad," she told us the second night.

"Because that way you can't even smell it, and smelling things is a huge part of tasting them."

"Yes, that's what the Freds taught us, back at the Fredtown school," Rosi said wearily. I could see her making an effort to smile at Cana through her exhaustion.

"Yes, you need to eat the food from the trough, just like the rest of us, so you don't starve," I said. "I bet Alcibiades would insist on that, too."

"Yes, he did say to eat," Cana agreed cheerfully. "He said his planet used to be known for having the best food in the galaxy, and he apologized for not being able to serve me pickled Alley-oops or candied Zeli-oots. He said once you eat those delicacies, you never forget."

How did a five-year-old know a word like "delicacy"?

"So Alcibiades is from this planet?" Edwy asked.

"Oh yes," Cana said. "He says his people were the first ones the Enforcers . . . enslaved. He said his people were really sad when the Enforcers began bringing others here to torture too."

"What's 'enslaved' mean?" Rosi asked in a whisper. "What's 'torture'?"

"What's happening to us, stupid," Enu told her.

How could Cana, a mere five-year-old, understand concepts like that, when twelve-year-old Rosi seemed never to have heard of them?

For that matter, even Edwy had a blank expression on his face.

"Who taught you those words?" I asked Cana. My voice came out harsh and accusing. "'Enslaved'? 'Torture'?"

"Alcibiades," Cana said, blinking her green eyes innocently up at me. Her face seemed to be growing thinner and thinner—it made her eyes look huge.

"Oh, because of course someone who's from this planet, who's a total *alien*—of course he speaks the same language as humans do on Earth," Enu said sarcastically. "So he can explain big words to you. *That's* convenient too."

"No, Alcibiades doesn't speak the same language as me," Cana said, shaking her head emphatically. She giggled. "That would be silly. Because we *are* from different planets, and he didn't have Freds helping him grow up. No, he just showed me where to find a translator device. It hangs on the wall outside his prison cell. Then he showed me how to use it. That's how we can talk."

"Something like that would have to be electronic, right? You have to bring it to me," I said, forgetting for a moment that everything Cana said was just make-believe, a little girl's fantasy to help her cope with the horror of being imprisoned and alone all day long. "Bring it to me, and I can rewire it, and I can use it to send a signal into outer space, a call for help. . . ."

Cana tilted her head to the side, deliberating.

"That *sounds* like a good idea," she said. "But Alcibiades says I have to put the translator back in the exact same place every afternoon before I come back here. Because the Enforcers come and check on them every night. If I took the translator device, the Enforcers would know. They might even come and punish you."

"But—" I began.

Enu slugged me in the shoulder.

"This is all pretend, remember?" he half whispered, half snarled in my ear. "Don't waste your energy getting all excited about having a new electronic device to play with. What she's talking about? It doesn't even exist!"

"Yeah, I know," I admitted sadly.

Just thinking about an electronic device had made my hands itch with longing. Without even thinking about it, I pulled out my mobile phone and began patting its screen. If only . . .

My gaze fell on the pebble I'd managed to smuggle in the first day, which we left with Cana every morning. We circled around it like it was a fireplace every evening. It seemed miraculous that it was still glowing.

"Wait—that pebble is some kind of power source, right?" I asked Enu. "What if I figure out some way to link up my phone and the pebble? Probably all I need is some extra wire, and then . . ."

"You are not breaking our only light!" Enu shouted at me with so much force I had to blink back tears. Big, tough, fifteen-year-old Enu was still afraid of the dark?

Well, yeah, so am I right now. . . .

What would we do when this pebble burned out?

"You guys, we have to try harder than ever to find a way to bring another pebble down here," I told the others. "And, Cana, when you're wandering around on your way to visit— what's his name? Alcibiades?—look for any spare wire or cord you can find, anything I could use to hook my phone to. . . ."

"And why don't you teach Alcibiades your language, and have him teach you yours?" Rosi told Cana. "That will give you both something fun to do, and it will show respect for each other's cultures."

Enu rolled his eyes at me.

"You know none of this is any good," he said. "If there was any life on this planet, any time in history, they're all dead now. And we're going to be too, soon. Don't you see how skinny we're all getting?"

At least he had the grace to keep his voice down, so I was the only one who heard.

"We'll be fine," I told him. "We *are* going to figure out a way to escape."

But days passed—weeks? Maybe a whole month?—and nothing changed except Cana's fanciful stories every night.

And the fact that, as Enu had pointed out, all of us kept getting skinnier and skinnier. The pebble's light didn't burn out, but none of us managed to smuggle another pebble down into our prison cell. I couldn't decide: Did the Enforcers know we had the pebble, and they didn't bother taking it away because we were trapped regardless? Or did they neither know nor care, and they never watched us underground—because we were trapped regardless?

All my thoughts led back to being trapped. We couldn't figure out how to get past the door down the hallway that was locked every night. We couldn't figure out any other way to escape either.

And then one morning, something did change. I awoke when Enu's elbow dug into my ribs as he rose to his feet. I could tell by the way he moved that he was under the Enforcers' control. Quickly I grabbed Cana's hand and turned it over so the pebble bled light throughout the cell. Enu, Edwy, and Rosi were all marching toward the feeding trough. We'd all been sleeping piled up together so Cana would know to wake up and eat too, but she moved more groggily—more like a normal child awakened too soon and stumbling sleepily toward breakfast.

Only I still lay on the floor.

"Wait—what just happened?" I asked, almost as panicked by *not* having the Enforcers controlling me as I'd ever been by them taking control. "Are they having us work in shifts now? Am I going to have to go out there all by myself?"

Enu, Edwy, and Rosi continued strutting toward the feeding trough as if they hadn't heard me. But Cana whirled around and threw her arms around my shoulder.

"Alcibiades said this might happen someday!" she cried joyfully even as she hugged me tight. "I didn't know you'd be the first one!"

"What are you talking about?" I asked, blinking stupidly. "What's going on?"

"You get to stay the whole day with me!" Cana announced. "You finally get to meet Alcibiades!"

CHAPTER
TWENTY-SIX

"Um, okay," I said weakly. I sat up, and everything went momentarily black. I swayed, almost falling back to the floor.

Cana grabbed my shoulder.

"Oh, oh—you have to eat first!" she cried. "Because Alcibiades says if one of you gets to stay home with me, it's probably because you're not getting enough food!"

"Food, right," I said. It occurred to me that every morning when we all stood at the food trough, Cana stood by me, and so whatever she ate came out of my share. So maybe I had been getting less than everyone else.

All of us had been hungry constantly since we'd gotten to the prison, so it hadn't even seemed that noticeable.

If I ate now, would it be like I was taking food away from one of the others?

I let Cana tug me over toward the food trough, but it was much harder to eat the nasty, slimy concoction when I had control over my own mouth and throat, my own ability to chew and swallow.

"Come on, you *have* to," Cana whispered. "That's what all of you told me!"

I bent over the swill and pretended to lick it up. Mostly I was just trying not to vomit.

It was so weird to have control over eating again.

Quickly the food was gone, and Enu, Edwy, and Rosi turned toward the gap in the prison cell walls, toward the hallway leading out to the stairs.

"Now that there are two of us, maybe we can stop them!" I told Cana as I reached for Enu.

"I don't think so," Cana said sadly. "Don't you remember how I tried before?"

I circled my fingers around Enu's wrist, but he yanked away from me as if I didn't even exist. I wanted to scream, *Look at me! I'm your sister! I'm trying to help! You fight too!* But of course that was ridiculous. Enu had no control of his body.

And did I really want to do anything that might attract the Enforcers' attention?

Why would they even care if I live or die, if I'm not working for them digging up pebbles? I thought, and shivered.

My chance to hold on to Enu—or Edwy or Rosi—slipped away, just that quickly.

"Don't we have to hurry?" I asked Cana. "So we get out of the prison cell before the bars close again?"

"All the prison doors stay wide open during the day," Cana told me. "We don't have to do anything in a hurry."

"Oh," I said.

Enu, Edwy, and Rosi were in the hall now, and turning toward the stairs. Their every move was regimented and precise, perfectly in step.

"Did you ever try to follow us?" I asked Cana. "If I went up those stairs right now, could I slip out the door?"

My heart pounded at the thought of the Enforcer who stood at the top of the stairs every morning. Could I take him by surprise and knock him out?

For a moment I could see in my mind how this would work: I would be like an action hero in one of Enu's video games from back home. I'd give the Enforcer one karate chop in the back of the neck, and he'd crumple to the ground.

I tried to lift my arm. It trembled so badly, I had to use all my strength just to hold it a few inches out from my side.

In my mind's eye I saw myself crumpling at the Enforcer's feet before he even noticed me standing there.

I didn't dare follow Enu, Edwy, and Rosi out where the Enforcers would see how weak I was.

"There's, like, an invisible wall that blocks the stairs from me every day after everyone leaves," Cana told me. "Alcibiades says it's a pressure lock, just part of the security system. It will block you, too."

I felt strangely relieved that I couldn't try to be an action hero.

"But do you think one of the Enforcers will come down

to check on me when I don't show up at the top of the stairs?"
I asked.

Cana shrugged.

"They never came to check on *me*," she said. "Alcibiades
says if a person is too little or too young or too weak to work
very well, the Enforcers don't care what happens to them.
Because Enforcers aren't very nice."

I knew Alcibiades was imaginary—so how had Cana managed to figure all that out by herself? Once again she stunned
me by sounding too mature for a five-year-old. But it wasn't
like I knew dozens of five-year-olds to compare her with.

"Come *on*," Cana said, tugging on my arm. "Let's go see
Alcibiades."

I stumbled after her. My head felt woozy. Maybe I wasn't
just hungry. Maybe I was sick. Really sick.

It was hard to tell, because I'd felt sick with fear ever since
we'd arrived on this planet.

We reached the other side of the prison cell, and just as
Cana had predicted, the bars stayed in place, letting us slip
out easily. This was especially helpful, since I didn't feel like
trying to outrun anything. I felt like I'd used up most of my
energy just crossing the cell.

"Alcibiades says he has lots and lots of stories to share
with us," Cana said. "He'll probably have a new one just
for you!"

"That's . . . nice," I said dimly. I was mostly focused on putting one foot in front of the other.

After what felt like an eon or two, we reached the prison cell where we'd found Cana that first night.

The solid door that had stopped us from walking on down the hall that night stood wide open.

"Oh," I murmured. "You weren't making up that part of your story."

"Of course not," Cana said, laughing. "When I make up stories and tell people about them, I *say* they're just make-believe!"

"Uh-huh," I said.

I stepped past the door that had stopped us before. In the glow from the pebble light, the hallway ahead of us looked just like the one behind us: full of empty prison cells.

"Yeah, that was worth the walk," I muttered.

My head throbbed. I put my hand on Cana's shoulder to steady myself.

"Okay, this has been interesting, but if it's all more of the same ahead of us, maybe I'll go back to our prison cell and sleep the rest of the day," I told Cana. "Then, after that, maybe I can come up with a plan; maybe I'll figure out . . ."

I couldn't even put the words together to say what I needed to figure out.

"But Alcibiades wanted to meet you most of all!" Cana

said, grabbing my hand and pulling me forward. "I told him how good you were at using your mobile phone to find us a safe place to hide, back on Earth."

"I am? You did?" I asked. I was a little touched that Cana even remembered me leading everyone to safety, back in Refuge City.

Well, what we'd thought would be safety.

It was easier to let Cana keep pulling me on than to summon the energy to turn around. For several paces I just trudged forward, my gaze trained on the floor.

"You *will* be nice to Alcibiades even though he looks different, right?" Cana asked anxiously. "You know he's my friend."

"Sure," I muttered.

Maybe I'd be less dizzy if I looked straight ahead, instead of down? Maybe that would make me feel less like I was about to fall over and smash my face against the floor?

I lifted my head, the motion making me dizzy all over again. The hallway curved ahead, and the stones directly in front of me were coated in some sort of mold or mildew or fungus. It was probably some life-form we didn't even have on Earth.

"You would have kept me from running into that, right?" I muttered to Cana.

She didn't answer. She broke away, running past the curved wall and crying out, "Alcibiades! Alcibiades! Look who came with me!"

I turned to follow her. And there, for the first time, was a prison cell that didn't have any gaps in the bars . . . and *wasn't* empty. The vast, barred cell ahead of me teemed with . . . Were those giant slugs? Overgrown air-breathing polliwogs? Mutant squid? Even with the bright light of the pebble Cana carried, it was hard to make sense of what I was seeing. My mind tried out classifications: *Amphibians? Reptiles? Giant paramecia?* Then I settled on the proper word: *Aliens. These creatures are aliens.*

One of the slugs/polliwogs/squid/aliens let out a bellow that sounded like a dying moose.

"He says he's happy to see you!" Cana reported, patting a—what would you call it? A tentacle?—that one of the slugs stuck out through the bars of the prison cell. "Alcibiades, meet Kiandra! Kiandra, meet Alcibiades!"

Alcibiades wasn't imaginary. He'd never been imaginary. He was just . . .

Horrifying.

The floor rose up to meet my head, and everything went black.

CHAPTER
TWENTY-SEVEN

I came back to consciousness as something wet and slimy slithered up my arm. I heard the dying moose sound again, followed by a chorus of grunts and groans. The whole prison cell full of slugs—dozens of them, or maybe even *hundreds*— seemed to be crying out.

Correction: The whole prison cell full of slugs, plus *Cana*, who was making dying-moose groans and grunts of her own.

"Yes, yes, of course—I'll get the translator," she said, switching back to human language.

I turned my head to see her pull a small black device down from the wall. The grunts and groans and moans faded into background noise, and I heard a mechanical voice say, "I *think* this one is a human child too, but it's hard to tell with alien species. . . ."

"Yes, Kiandra is a kid, but she's a *big* kid, almost an adult, and I'm just a little kid," Cana said. Now the translation device let out a stream of grunts and groans, turning her words into slug language.

The slimy thing on my arm took hold and pulled me closer to the prison bars. I shrieked, and the slug creatures let out a series of dismayed clicks and clacks and groans. Even without the translation I could tell: They didn't want to be close to me any more than I wanted to be close to them.

A wave seemed to move through the prison cell, as most of the slug creatures pressed toward the back wall, trying to get as far away from me as possible.

Now, for the first time, I could see the slug creature who was touching me as an individual, not just one part of a giant lump of sliminess bulging with tentacles. He (she? It?) stood completely apart—or maybe crouched completely apart, kneeling on two of its four legs. (Did the appendages still count as legs if they ended in suction cups rather than feet?)

"Alcibiades, please—can you help Kiandra?" Cana asked, bending down beside me.

The translator put her words into the dying-moose tones of the slug language, and this set off another round of horrified grunts and groans and bellows from the pile of sliminess trying to escape the horror of me. My ears rang, and I missed the translation. But then the slug holding on to me— Alcibiades, I guess—replied in a firm, clear voice, and that silenced the others so thoroughly that the translation broke through the fog in my brain.

"If I want to spend my dying breath trying to save another creature—even an alien creature—what concern is that of yours?" Alcibiades asked. "I still have that choice left to me, do I not? When every other freedom has been taken away from me by the Enforcers, why would you deny me this decision as well? Allow me this one moment of independence!"

I turned my head toward Cana.

"I think I like your friend Alcibiades," I whispered. I didn't add that I liked him a lot better when I didn't actually have to look at him. I didn't have the breath for that and, well, even I knew how to be a little diplomatic.

The horrified grunts and groans turned into a wave of sounds that seemed a lot more like cheering.

When I turned my head back toward the cage full of slug creatures, two more had slithered up beside Alcibiades. They were also reaching tentacles toward me, and I instinctively jerked back.

Alcibiades spoke, and the translator kicked in simultaneously this time: "Don't be afraid. It appears that you have the Zacadi flu. But we can heal you. It won't hurt."

Maybe the translation device was glitchy. Or "healing" was code for "sliming." All three slug creatures rubbed tentacles on my arms, legs, and—ugh, ugh, ugh!—face, and it was like being bathed in raw egg. But oddly, my skin seemed to absorb the slime almost instantly.

The throbbing in my head disappeared. I sat up and didn't feel even a moment of dizziness. I propped my arms behind me, and not a single muscle gave off a twinge of achy protest.

"You are immune now," Alcibiades told me, the translator making sense of his words instantly. "You will never suffer from the Zacadi flu again."

I stared into his face—or at least I tried to. It was possible that his eyes were located on the very top of his head.

"I—thank you," I said. "I feel better than I have in weeks. But . . . what *is* the Zacadi flu? I've never heard of it."

I heard the rumble of the translator along with my words, but it was getting easier and easier to tune that out when I was speaking, and tune out everything *but* the translator when Alcibiades and his fellow slugs spoke.

"Zacadi—that is our planet," Alcibiades said. "Did no one tell you?" He seemed to be gazing down at Cana, a frightful movement that meant his eyes slid downward until they were roughly where the jaw would be, on a human.

Part of me was still marveling at how Alcibiades had cured me. But, evilly, I was also wishing I could get Enu and Alcibiades together, to see how much big, tough Enu would shriek in terror at the slip-sliding eyes and slithering tentacles.

"Cana, did you not tell your friends everything, like I suggested?" Alcibiades asked. The translator made him sound like a stern schoolmaster.

"I *tried*," Cana said. "But they didn't always listen very well. I think they were all too tired from working too hard all day."

And we didn't believe you, I thought guiltily.

"Ah, I can understand that level of exhaustion," Alcibiades said, and even before the translator kicked in, I could hear the weight of sorrow in his voice. He looked directly at me now, his eyes rolling back to the middle of his head. "Our planet is Zacadi, and we are known as the Zacadian people. We are . . . interconnected with our planet . . . and because the Enforcers destroy our planet as they take away our Zacadi pearls, we are dying off."

"Zacadi pearls?" I asked.

Alcibiades pointed to the pebble glowing in Cana's hand.

"Our . . . energy source," he said. "Our life force."

"The Enforcers are taking them away, and that's killing you?" I asked.

"It's not that, exactly, but . . ." Alcibiades's eyes slid in Cana's direction again. "Cana, perhaps you and Melos and Arkan can work on your Zacadian language lessons, while I tell Kiandra everything I've already told you," he suggested gently.

"Okay," Cana said. She fiddled with the translator for a second, then handed it to me. "You can use this. I'll practice without it."

She sat down at the other end of the prison bars. The two other slug creatures—no, Zacadians—who'd slimed—er, healed—me slithered toward her with softly bellowed greetings. Apparently Cana had set the translator to work only within a narrow range, because it didn't provide an interpretation. Alcibiades waited until all of them had started a pattern of back-and-forth grunting and groaning before he spoke again.

"It is a long and sad story," he said. "It is hard for me to gauge the age and maturation levels of alien creatures. You do not look much bigger than Cana. When do your people become adults?"

"Trust me, I'm close enough," I said.

I think I was learning to interpret Zacadian facial expressions; Alcibiades looked doubtful.

But he sighed and curled his tentacle-like legs beneath him. We stared at each other from opposite sides of the prison bars.

"Then I will tell you the entirety of the truth, which I did not tell Cana," he said, and I thought I could detect the weight of grief in his voice again. "We Zacadians invented the Zacadi flu ourselves. To kill our very own brothers and sisters. But, I swear, we never knew where it would lead."

"Which is . . . ," I prompted.

His eyes did not seem so foreign anymore. They only seemed sad.

"Every other Zacadian who ever lived is dead now," he whispered. "Every Zacadian . . . except the ones in this prison cell. And soon we will be dead too. Our entire species will be extinct. And it will be our own fault."

CHAPTER
TWENTY-EIGHT

"But how . . . ?" I began.

Alcibiades held up one of his upper tentacles, and I was pretty sure the motion was like a human holding up a hand to indicate, *No, no, let me talk now. You just listen.*

"I am ashamed to tell this story," he whispered.

"Yes, my people—humans, those of us from Earth—we have a lot to be ashamed of too," I said.

Alcibiades bowed the blob at the top of his body that seemed to correlate to a human head.

"Then perhaps you can understand that we are not like the Enforcers?" he asked. "Enforcers do not feel shame, and when they came here, well . . ."

"Then maybe this is all their fault, not yours?" I asked, with an eagerness that made me sound almost as young as Cana. It felt as if convincing Alcibiades that his people had actually done nothing wrong would make humans seem less guilty too.

"But that is not true," Alcibiades said with another heavy sigh.

"Please, can you just start at the beginning?" I asked.

"The beginning . . . ," Alcibiades repeated. "My people and my planet were rich and proud and happy. The Zacadi pearls—even you have seen that they are a marvel, correct?"

"Yes," I said.

"And all you know is that they give light and never burn out," Alcibiades said with a shrug.

"Well, I *suspected* that there was more to them, but we only had the one, so we were afraid to experiment much." I paused. "Are you sure they never burn out? What I remember from science class—is that even possible? Perpetual energy machines are just fantasies, aren't they?"

"*Maybe* Zacadi pearls can burn out, but no Zacadian has lived long enough to witness such a thing," Alcibiades conceded.

"Do they just occur naturally on your planet?" I asked. "Or did your people invent them?"

"Our people have many stories about where they came from, and why they are buried in our soil," Alcibiades said. "Do those stories even matter now? Call them a gift of nature. No Zacadian remembers a time when the pearls were not part of our lives."

"Limitless energy, always available," I said. "You live on a lucky planet."

"The planet may still be lucky, but we are not," Alcibiades murmured.

"What changed?" I asked. "You were rich and proud and happy and then . . ." It seemed really rude to point out that he and all his people were confined to a prison cell now, with no possessions whatsoever, as far as I could tell.

A shudder passed through Alcibiades, unsettling every tentacle.

"My people advanced quickly to the point of space exploration," he said. "We had so much power and energy at our disposal—spaceships were toys for us."

"What's wrong with that?" I asked.

"When I told Cana this story, she said it sounded like toddlers getting their own cars," he said. "Then she had to explain what a car was. My people skipped that stage of development and went straight to airplanes and flying."

"Cana meant toddlers would crash cars, right?" I said. "So . . . did your people have a lot of spaceship accidents?"

I'm pretty sure the look Alcibiades gave me was both baffled and indignant. But it was a little hard to interpret such an alien creature's face, with such constantly rolling eyes and rippling, slimy skin. It may have been that his actual mouth was located where a human stomach would be, but I couldn't even be sure of that.

"No, of course we didn't have lots of spaceship accidents,"

Alcibiades said. "Our technology wasn't flawed. Just our . . . souls."

"What do souls have to do with spaceships?" I asked.

Alcibiades drew away from me. He peered at the translator in my hands as if he didn't trust it.

"Spaceships meant we encountered other civilizations," he said slowly, as if giving the words time to sink in. "Before we were ready. We were too . . . chaotic and undisciplined. Do you know the primary rule of the intergalactic court regarding primitive civilizations? There must be no interference on any planet until and unless that planet's intelligent-life species develops space travel. That is because encountering other civilizations before one is ready is too disruptive, too disorienting. We weren't ready to choose."

"Choose?" I echoed. "Choose what?"

"Surely you know that the intergalactic court preserves a balance between the two types of advanced civilizations present in the universe," Alcibiades said.

"It does?" I asked.

Alcibiades recoiled again.

"Your people *have* ventured out into space, correct?" he asked. "Apart from being enslaved on my planet?"

"Ye-es," I mumbled. "Probably the leaders of my planet know all about the intergalactic court. But I am a thirteen-year-old girl who . . . Oh, never mind. Don't tell me how ignorant I am. Teach me what you know."

I swear Alcibiades's expression was admiring now.

"Ah, so your people—even their youth—are capable of wisdom," he murmured.

He made a sound that might have been the equivalent of humans clearing their throats before launching into a long speech.

"One category of civilizations represented on the intergalactic court is best embodied by the people popularly known as Freds," Alcibiades said. "The peace lovers. The kind ones. The gentle saints. The ones who want to do nothing but help."

I was about to protest, but Alcibiades kept talking.

"The Enforcers and the others like them make up the second type of civilization," Alcibiades. "They are grim and austere, and they began in chaotic violence. But as mature civilizations, they exercise iron control over themselves. And over others. They limit their violent impulses to enforcing the rules of the intergalactic court. They still enjoy violence, but they only indulge their love of violence in the service of keeping the universe peaceful."

I leaped to my feet and grabbed the prison bars before me.

"You're saying the intergalactic court *knows* about everything the Enforcers do?" I ask. "They know my friends and I are stuck here as slaves? They know we're slowly being starved and worked to death? They know your people are going extinct? And they approve of that?"

Tremors flowed through Alcibiades's entire body. Maybe he was crying. The mound of his fellow Zacadians quaked behind him. Maybe they were all sobbing.

"The—the Enforcers tell us they have full authorization to do what they do here," Alcibiades stammered. "No other species has come to tell us otherwise. So why should I doubt them? What my people did . . . we got greedy and started selling our Zacadi pearls far and wide. And then we fought over the Zacadi pearls, and one group of Zacadians invented the Zacadi flu to kill off their enemies, who wanted the pearl profits for themselves. We destroyed our entire planet."

"Okay, maybe the *individuals* who did those things deserved punishment," I told Alcibiades. "But were *babies* involved in the killing? Were little children?" I was getting dangerously close to crying myself. I almost veered into explaining how wrong it was that the so-called saintly Freds chose to save baby Edwy but left one-year-old me behind on dangerous Earth. So how were the Freds any better than the Enforcers?

Instead I pointed at Cana, still obliviously practicing grunts and groans while the slug creature on the other side of the bars from her patted her head gently with one of his tentacles.

"Does that little girl from my planet deserve to die in this alien place because *my* parents murdered some of their neighbors more than a decade ago?"

Alcibiades stared at me through the bars as though the translator had broken down. As though he couldn't understand anything I'd said. But I could hear the mechanical grunts and groans and clicks resounding after every single one of my words—it *seemed* like my question had been translated.

Then the ripples flowing up and down on Alcibiades's head smoothed out.

"No," he finally whispered. "She does not deserve to die. Neither do you. Neither . . . do I."

He began wrapping tentacles around the same bars I held, as if he needed the support to stay upright.

"If the Freds let Cana die, they're as guilty as the Enforcers," I said. "The entire intergalactic court is at fault. They're *all* evil."

Alcibiades still had an expression on his face that looked like astonishment.

"Yes," he said. "But what can we do about it?"

I stared at the bars between us, and the way my tightly gripped hands were surrounded above and below by his tentacles.

No—not just surrounded. Accompanied. Linked. The bars and our completely different anatomy didn't really separate us that much. We were connected too.

"We work together," I said. "To save all the Zacadian and human lives we can."

Alcibiades's face rippled again, but only once before the motion subsided and his expression froze in place again. Maybe it was like a human raising a single eyebrow.

"My people are still good at spaceships," he said. "What are your people good at?"

CHAPTER
TWENTY-NINE

"You're delusional," Enu said. "You were hallucinating."

Cana and I were back in our prison cell, back with the other three. It was evening again, and Enu, Edwy, and Rosi had just come marching back down the stairs and collapsed at our feet. Maybe I should have given them a moment to untangle their arms and legs and sit up before I'd started excitedly telling the story of meeting Alcibiades and making a plan to escape.

But it felt like every moment that passed without doing something was a waste.

"Do you still feel sick?" Rosi asked.

She made an effort to shove herself up from the floor and reach a hand toward my forehead, as if to feel for a fever. I jerked away, and she almost toppled over.

Maybe she would be next to be deemed too unhealthy to go out to work. Maybe she had the Zacadi flu already.

Then Alcibiades and the others would cure her, I told

myself. *Then she could help me and Alcibiades and the others down here in the prison. . . .*

And then the Enforcers would give us even less food. Alcibiades had explained how that worked too. None of his people were considered healthy enough to work anymore, so they were given only starvation rations. And their cell was kept locked, day and night, so they had no hope of escaping on their own.

I thought about one of the other facts that he'd told me that he hadn't shared with Cana: The reason the Enforcers came to the Zacadians' prison cell every night—but not to ours—was to check for dead bodies to be removed. That wasn't necessary in our prison cell. Not yet.

But someday, if we don't escape soon . . .

I pushed that thought out of my mind.

"I feel fine," I told Rosi, sounding much harsher than I intended. "Never been better."

"Kiandra, you're a skeleton," Enu said. He stood up, towering over me, using his height like a weapon to beat me down. "It's your own fault. You should have eaten more back on Earth, when you had the chance, instead of skipping meals to work on your computer all day. And now . . . And now . . . you're not even making sense!"

He was almost yelling. Tears stung at my eyes. How were we ever going to be able to unite with the Zacadians against the Enforcers if I couldn't even talk my own brother into working with me?

"I think he's only mad and being mean because he's worried about you," Rosi offered. "Back in Fredtown, sometimes when Edwy was mean to me, my Fred-mama would say—"

"Stop talking about the Freds!" Enu commanded.

He was shaking.

"Enu, are *you* sick?" I asked.

"Sick of being here," he said. "Sick of knowing there's nothing we can do to get away. Sick of those Enforcers using my muscles—the muscles *I* worked so hard to build—and now I can't even punch that Enforcer who stands at the top of the stairs every morning and stares at me all day; I can't even fight the urge to dig and dig and dig, all day long, I can't even—"

"Enu, we all feel that way," Edwy said. And it was odd: *He* sounded calm and rational. Like he was the older brother, the more mature one, and Enu was a little kid throwing a tantrum. "So why don't you listen to Kiandra?"

"Because I can't let her get my hopes up again!" Enu screamed. "Because . . . you want to tell me about some crazy aliens and their fantasy spaceship? If those, those *animals* you think you saw have some old, broken-down spaceship somewhere, I'm sure the Enforcers have something bigger and fancier and faster. Something that could shoot us out of the sky in an instant. . . . It's no good!"

"Except the Enforcers didn't use a spaceship to send us here, remember?" I countered. "That's not how they got here either. They think of spaceships as old technology. Alcibiades says the Enforcers have been here so long, and the Zacadians have just been prisoners for so long, that the Enforcers stopped worrying about anyone escaping in a Zacadian spaceship ages ago. They've gotten lazy. They—"

"Even lazy, they can control every move my body makes!" Enu exploded. "If the spaceship's so old, how's it going to work?" He clutched his head in his hands. "There you go again, making me think . . . making me think . . ."

Abruptly he sat back down. He spun around, facing away from all of us. His shoulders shook.

Was Enu crying? Enu?

I looked down at my own hands. They were bonier than ever. I looked back up. Edwy, Rosi, and Cana were all staring at me, their eyes huge in their shrunken faces. And their faces *were* shrunken. I needed to pay attention to that now.

For all his bragging about muscles, even Enu was scrawnier than I'd ever seen him.

His shoulders kept heaving up and down.

"I don't think we have much time," I said quietly. "We can't waste it arguing. We need to . . . conserve our energy."

"For what?" Edwy asked. "How would the plan work?"

"Yes, tell us," Rosi echoed. "I want you to give us hope. I—I don't think I can live without it."

"*We must accept finite disappointment, but never lose infinite hope*," Cana chirped. "Martin Luther King Jr. said that. It was a principle of—"

She glanced nervously at Enu's back and clapped her hand over her mouth. I guessed the next word was supposed to be "Fredtown."

"And *Everything that is done in the world is done by hope*," Edwy said. "I think Martin Luther King said that one too."

"No, it was Martin Luther," Rosi corrected. "Different people. But still, Edwy—*you're* quoting one of the principles of Fredtown?"

Then she glanced nervously in Enu's direction as well.

This time he did whirl around. But he threw up his arms, rather than punch anyone.

"Okay, okay!" he cried. "You've beat me down. I'll do whatever Kiandra wants. I'll even work with slugs. Just stop talking about hope and Fredtown!"

CHAPTER THIRTY

In the morning, I woke when my body stood up on its own. Every other morning it had been horrifying to lose control, but today I wanted to jump up and down and pump my fist in the air and shout: *Yes! Yes! Yes!* Evidently the Enforcers thought I was healthy enough to dig again. That meant I would get to try the technique Alcibiades had recommended for smuggling more Zacadi pearls away from the Enforcers— the first step in the plan we'd come up with for escape. I wouldn't have to rely on Enu, Edwy, and Rosi to do that part.

Of course, I couldn't jump up and down or shout. Instead my body moved automatically toward the feeding trough. Every other morning when I'd lost control, I'd fought it, my brain crying out to my limbs, *No, no—stop that! Don't do what the Enforcers want you to do! Stop walking. Stop eating that horrible slop. Resist!* I'd worn myself out fighting the Enforcers' control, and the only thing I had to show for it was a single Zacadi pearl and several weeks' worth of starvation and exhaustion.

What Alcibiades had told me to do was to stop resisting. To cooperate.

"The Enforcers expect you to fight back, so they compensate for that," he'd said. "If they want you to move your hand to the right and *you* try to move your hand to the right at the same time, your hand goes too far. So then they have to set lower levels of control, and you have a chance to steal a Zacadi pearl. You just have to become unpredictable, cooperating sometimes, resisting sometimes."

I was enough like Enu that I'd asked suspiciously, "If this works so well, why didn't your people grab dozens of Zacadi pearls a long time ago and escape on your own?"

Alcibiades wouldn't meet my eye.

"Because whenever we managed to get a Zacadi pearl, we didn't try to use it for escape," he said. "We used it to try to kill Enforcers. Our aim was nothing but revenge. Why do you think the Enforcers stay so separate from us prisoners most of the time? Why do you think my people are no longer sent out to dig for Zacadi pearls?"

I was still trying to figure out the Enforcers.

"But they didn't try to kill *you* to get revenge for your revenge," I said. "That's, um . . ."

I couldn't make myself say what I was thinking, *That's what humans would do if they had the powers Enforcers have.*

Then Alcibiades raised his head and peered sadly at me.

"Don't you think the way my people are dying now is worse than instant death?" he asked. "Don't you see how they're torturing us, making us watch one another die? Making us watch our own deaths coming toward us?"

If Enu, Edwy, Rosi, and I tried the method Alcibiades suggested for getting Zacadi pearls, how long would that take? How long before the Enforcers caught on to what we were doing?

How long did we have left to survive, anyhow?

I pushed all those questions out of my mind and focused on how my feet were walking me toward the feeding trough along the wall. Left, right, left, right . . .

I'm really hungry, I told myself. *I am dying to get to that delicious food.*

The "delicious" part was crazy, but I fooled myself into putting extra oomph into picking up my left foot, kicking it straight out, planting it on the floor, and shoving off again.

I stumbled, tripped forward, and felt my body only barely manage to catch itself—er, myself—before I fell against the wall.

How many Zacadians ended up with broken bones or concussions when they tried this? I wondered. My head had barely missed smashing into one of the bricks. *Why didn't Alcibiades tell me that?*

Maybe the Zacadians didn't even have bones in their bodies. Maybe they couldn't get concussions.

I plunged my face forward, driving my chin down as the Enforcers' control of my body bent my neck. My chin slammed into the hard edge of the trough.

Enu will laugh at me when I have a bruise later on, I thought. *He's probably managing to do this without injuring himself.*

My mouth landed in the gruel, and my head automatically turned to the left to gobble up a glob off to the side. This meant I could gaze toward the spot where Enu had stood to eat every other morning.

He wasn't there.

My head turned again, left to right to left again, and I shoved it as far as I could in either direction as my tongue methodically licked up the gruel.

Rosi and Edwy were missing too.

Even if they're sick like I was yesterday, they still would have come over to the trough, I thought. *But, but . . .*

The Enforcers chose that moment to make me focus on eating the food directly below my mouth. I couldn't turn my head in any direction. My mind spun.

Maybe everyone else is just still sleeping?

No—there was light to see by, and that meant Cana was awake and had taken the Zacadi pearl out of her pocket. And once she was awake, even if the others were sick like I was yesterday, she would have poked and prodded and tugged them over to the feeding trough just as she'd done for me.

Even Cana hadn't come over to the feeding trough.

It was agony to stand still and keep eating and eating and eating when all I wanted to do was whirl around and look for my brothers and the two other girls. What had happened to them?

Finally, after what seemed like an eternity, the trough was empty. My back straightened up and my body turned. I threw my energy into turning completely—cooperating completely—in hopes that the action would give me a moment of extra control. I just needed to be able to look down for a second, to see . . .

My eyes could only look forward, toward the gap in the bars that led out into the hallway.

Just then I felt someone tugging on my shirt.

"Kiandra! Kiandra!" It was Cana. "The others won't get up!"

The Enforcers didn't let me break stride; they kept my body moving quickly and efficiently past Cana. But they *finally* let me look down, because I had to step over three lumpy shapes on the floor: Enu, Edwy, and Rosi.

Why won't they move? I wondered. *Are they . . . are they even breathing?*

Just as my head began to snap back up, to gaze entirely forward again, I thought I caught the barest glimpse of Edwy's chest rising and falling, of Rosi's head turning slightly as a look of agony spread across her face.

But Enu? Is he—

I couldn't get my head to bend down again. I could see nothing but the bars and prison walls ahead of me. My feet carried me mercilessly forward, farther and farther away from the others.

Farther and farther away from finding out if my brother was alive or dead.

CHAPTER
THIRTY-ONE

For a long time, I could think only, *Enu! Enu! I have to find out about Enu!* Meanwhile, my body moved automatically out of the prison cell, down the hallway, up the stairs, out the door. I must have passed the Enforcer guard; I must have wrapped my fingers around the handle of a shovel. I could guess these things, because when I started paying attention again, I was digging the tip of a shovel into the ground and pulling up a pile of dirt. Then I crouched down and began methodically picking through the dirt, pulling out the round lumps of Zacadi pearls.

I was working alone. Off in the distance I could see other work teams, just as we had on other days. But the Enforcers had evidently decided it wasn't worth the bother to pair me up with any other workers.

This made me feel even worse, even lonelier, even more worried about Enu and the others.

I know Rosi and Edwy were breathing. So they're alive.

Enu was always stronger than any of us, so if they're alive, so is he. They probably all have the Zacadi flu, like I did yesterday, and Cana will take them to Alcibiades to be cured. They'll be able to get up for that. They'll be fine. Just like I'm fine now.

I wasn't fine. Even with my body under the Enforcers' control, my hands shook. I could barely get my fingers to press together well enough to grasp the Zacadi pearls I was supposed to pluck out of the dirt and drop into a nearby bucket.

How much longer do any of us have to live? What if none of us are healthy enough after today to come out and search for the pearls?

This could be the last chance any of us had for stealing the pearls we needed for our escape.

Was it my imagination, or were my hands shaking more than ever?

You're wasting time, I told myself, as harsh as any of the cruel nannies Enu and I had when we were little kids.

Enu . . .

I stopped letting myself think my brother's name. I focused on following the directions Alcibiades had given me, willing my hand to plunge into the dirt before me.

Even though Enu's the one who's good at physical things, not me . . . .

Had I lasted even two seconds managing not to think about Enu?

In my mind's eye, I saw myself as a little kid. I'd been five years old then—maybe six. Enu had gone out to play basketball, and he'd left with the taunt, "It's boys only, Kiandra! You can't follow me this time!" I'd cried and cried and cried, and then I'd grabbed a laptop because I got sick of hearing myself cry. And that was the day I took my first tutorial in coding. I fell into it so completely that when Enu came home and half apologized—"Maybe next time I'll see if they'll let girls play too"—I was able to retort, "Oh, were you away? I didn't even notice."

Well, yeah, it's easy to focus on digital things and shut out the whole rest of the world. Physical things . . . not so much.

But I concentrated my whole being on doing what the Enforcers wanted me to do: picking up a Zacadi pearl, dropping it in the bucket. Sliding a layer of dirt to the side, picking up another Zacadi pearl . . .

I plucked up twenty Zacadi pearls and all but threw them into the bucket.

On the twenty-first pearl, I faked out the Enforcers. As I passed my hand over my knee, I suddenly jerked back, letting the thumb and forefinger that held the pearl separate ever so slightly.

The Zacadi pearl bounced off my knee and dropped to the ground. It rolled away.

Go after it! My mind screamed. *Crawl over and . . .*

My hand kept moving toward the bucket. My fingers opened completely, as if the force controlling my body didn't realize I'd lost the pearl.

Interesting, I thought. Maybe the Enforcers weren't paying as much attention to me as it seemed.

I just had to try again.

The next time I moved twenty-three pearls in a row while my brain cooperated entirely with what the Enforcers wanted me to do. On the twenty-fourth pearl, I managed to use my left hand to pull out the top of my shorts pocket as my right hand lifted a pearl toward the bucket. And then I darted my right hand back toward my shorts and let go of the pearl.

The pearl fell straight down into my pocket.

My face flushed with victory—or exertion. My brain felt like I'd just finished a six-hour calculus exam; my body felt like I'd just run a marathon. If I'd had total control of myself at that point, I would have fallen over in exhaustion.

But the Enforcers drove me to keep picking up pearls and dropping them in the bucket.

Okay, okay, go back to cooperating, I reminded myself. *And then steal another pearl.*

If the calculations Alcibiades had done were correct, I only had to succeed seven more times.

CHAPTER THIRTY-TWO

By the end of the day, it was a race between me and the setting sun. I had six Zacadi pearls in my pocket (and I had probably let three times that many roll off to the side after failed efforts to snag them). Whenever the Enforcers let me lift my head at all, I cast an anxious eye toward the glow in the overcast sky—did I still have another hour? Or was I down to a half hour? Or just fifteen minutes?

Every other day I'd longed for the Enforcers to stop my digging and propel me back toward my prison cell. But today I kept thinking, *Please let me stay out here longer. Please give me time to get two more pearls. . . .*

I took more risks now, only cooperating with the Enforcers for the time it took to pick up one or two Zacadi pearls before I tried to drop one in my pocket. But that only led to more failures.

Wait fifteen, I told myself. *Then try.*

It was agonizing to wait, especially since every muscle in my body ached. But I made myself be patient: *That's eleven pearls' worth of cooperation. . . . Twelve . . . Thirteen . . .*

Just as I started to reach for the fourteenth pearl, my back straightened up, my knees unbent, my foot kicked up to push me up into a standing position.

If I'd had power over my vocal cords, I would have forgotten myself and screamed, *No fair! I only have six pearls! And I need eight!*

Stiffly, my body stumbled back toward the door to the prison. I guess even the Enforcers couldn't make me walk in a straight line without swaying. The force of the water spraying me off almost knocked me over. Or maybe it just felt that way because I was so disappointed.

You can get the rest tomorrow. And probably the others will be healed and able to help you. You got six pearls in one day alone; surely four of us working a full day together can succeed in getting the last two. . . .

I stumbled down the stairs and into our prison cell. As soon as my body hit the floor I sprang back up, calling out, "Enu? Edwy? Rosi? Cana?"

All I heard in response was a groan. I looked down—Enu, Edwy, and Rosi were still lying on the floor. For all I could tell, they might not have moved at all since I'd left that morning.

Then I heard a sob: Cana. She was crouched against the wall, her face tear-streaked.

"I couldn't get them to get up," she wailed. "And I couldn't move them. . . . All I could do was run to Alcibiades, and he put slime on my hands and I brought it back to them and put it on their faces—I did it again and again and again. But it wasn't enough! Alcibiades said that would keep them alive until you got back, but . . . but . . ."

I dropped to my knees and pressed my fingers against Enu's neck.

"He still has a pulse." I breathed a sigh of relief and checked Edwy and Rosi as well. "They're all still alive. Cana, you saved all of them!"

"But the door will be locked now, and so we can't get to Alcibiades until morning, and tomorrow morning you'll be sent out again," Cana whined. I think I'd spent pretty much every moment of my fifth year whining, but this was the first time I'd heard such a sulky tone in her voice. "Any time you'll be here to help, the door will be locked!"

"Oh, but now I know how to unlock it," I told Cana. "We can take Enu, Edwy, and Rosi down to Alcibiades to be cured right now."

"How?" Cana moaned. "How can you unlock the door now when nobody could before?"

I reached into my shorts pocket and pulled out one of the precious Zacadi pearls I'd managed to steal. I held up the pearl, right before Cana's eyes. It seemed to glitter with power.

"We use this," I told Cana. "And we don't unlock anything. We blow it up."

CHAPTER THIRTY-THREE

Even working together, I knew Cana and I would have trouble pushing and pulling and tugging Enu, Edwy, and Rosi down the hall. We started with Rosi, and she should have been the lightest, but I still had trouble lifting her shoulders; Cana still had trouble lifting her feet. We bumped her spine on the hard stone floor with every step we took, and her head wobbled side to side, but she stayed silent.

"See how brave Rosi is!" Cana gasped. "She doesn't even complain!"

I couldn't take that as a good sign. It probably meant that she was too deeply ill to even feel the pain.

We left Rosi propped near the locked door in the hallway, and went back to retrieve Enu and Edwy.

"It might make a lot of noise when we blow the door open, and we'll have to move as fast as possible then, getting down to Alcibiades's cell," I told Cana. "So it's best if we have everyone as close as possible, first."

Cana nodded knowingly, but I wasn't sure she understood. I kind of wanted to scream at her, *Don't you see this is going to be impossible? Don't you see we can't possibly move Enu, Edwy, and Rosi all down to Alcibiades—and give them time to be cured enough to be able to run—and then blow out another wall and escape—all before the Enforcers hear us and come to capture us?*

Our plan would have been risky even if Enu, Edwy, and Rosi had been able to walk. Even if I'd had enough energy left for running.

But what else can we do except try?

I swayed walking back to our prison cell. I wasn't even carrying anybody now, and I was still having trouble moving forward instead of reeling into the walls. Or collapsing.

"Let's take Edwy next," I told Cana. "That way we can build our muscles and work our way up to dealing with heavy old Enu."

Didn't she see how that was totally backward—how we really should have taken Enu first, while we still had energy?

Cana squared her shoulders and walked faster. And there was nothing I could do but speed up behind her.

Edwy was no harder to carry/drag than Rosi had been, but I felt like crawling might be too much for me afterward. The weight of my phone in my back pocket felt like a huge burden. I could stay upright only because Cana was with me;

I could keep walking only because she walked beside me. I hoped she couldn't tell how wiped out I was, but just as we got back to our prison cell, she slipped her hand into mine.

"I bet we could roll Enu if we had to," she said. "The hallway's wide enough."

"Roll . . . ," I repeated dimly.

"You know," she said. "Like how we all used to roll down the little hill back in Fredtown, and our Fred-mommies and Fred-daddies used to give us a push to get us started . . . and everyone would laugh and laugh and laugh. . . . Oh, sorry. You don't know what it was like in Fredtown, do you?"

"No," I grunted.

I tried to imagine a place where kids laughed that much about silly stuff like rolling in the grass. Most of the laughter I remembered from back in Refuge City was from kids making fun of other kids, trying to make them feel bad.

And I remembered Enu laughing at me sometimes when I wanted to play with him and his friends, and he didn't want me to.

And now I'm saving your life, dude. You'd better be alert enough to notice and appreciate it!

I wanted that thought to make me fierce and strong. I wanted to be fury-powered. But I was doing well to put one foot in front of the other. I was doing well not to just fall over myself.

Cana was already bending down beside Enu, shoving on his shoulders. He flopped forward, his head lolling side to side.

Oh, Enu, please stay unconscious, I thought. *Because this is going to hurt. . . .*

It seemed to take a thousand years to roll Enu out of the cell and down the hall. We left him beside Rosi and Edwy, a good distance back from the door.

"You stand behind the other kids, to be safe," I told Cana as I stepped closer to the door.

"Shouldn't you be safe too?" Cana asked in a wobbly voice.

"I have to be close to the door to throw the Zacadi pearl," I said. "I have to put one on the floor and hit it by throwing a second one. But Alcibiades says it's almost like the pearls have their own brains—they'll know not to send the blast zone out farther than I'm standing when I throw the pearl."

I hoped Alcibiades was right.

I hoped a lot of things.

Cana stood back. I wedged one of the Zacadi pearls against the bottom of the door, then straightened up. I took two steps away, which was about as far as I could go and still be sure of my throwing accuracy.

"If this doesn't work . . . ," I began, pulling a second pearl out into my hand.

"Don't say that. It's going to work," Cana said behind me, as patiently as if she were the older one.

I lifted my arm and threw the Zacadi pearl to the floor. It seemed to arc to the side, but it still landed on the other pearl. I caught my breath. Nothing happened for a minute; then the door fell over backward, and the wall beside it crumbled down to nothing. Bits and pieces of concrete and metal soared toward me.

I scrambled backward, but the dodge was unnecessary: All the concrete and metal landed in a pile right before my feet.

"Okay, that was really impressive," I muttered.

"You did it!" Cana cried behind me.

I glanced back. The noise had roused Edwy and Rosi enough that they squirmed and moaned, but Enu remained deathly still.

That was definitely a bad sign.

"Hurry," I began, "let's get Enu to—"

But before I could move, I was hit with a second wave of sound, roaring into the shocked silence that had followed the explosion. This wasn't the rumble of more concrete and metal crumbling and falling. It was voices. *Human* voices. Screaming from the other side of the fallen door.

"What was that?"

"Who's there?"

"Has somebody come to save us? Help us! Please!"

CHAPTER THIRTY-FOUR

Quickly I scrambled past the rubble. At first I could see only darkness beyond the fallen door.

"Cana, the light—" I called over my shoulder.

The little girl was already climbing toward me, bringing her glowing Zacadi pearl with her. Once she reached the spot where the door had stood, the boundaries of the glow leaped forward, illuminating the hallway ahead, which was lined with rows of cages that had been completely empty the day before.

They weren't empty now. Each cage was packed with people. *Humans.* My first glance seemed to take in hundreds of shocked, upturned faces—men, women, and children all pleading with Cana and me, "Help! Set us free! Let us go! Do you know how we can get back to Earth?"

No—they weren't *all* pleading. Some were already moving through a destroyed corner of the cage nearest the fallen door. I'd evidently blown up the bars on that cage at the same time that I'd blown up the door.

I thought two things at once: *Just* look, *you ungrateful people! I* already *set you free! Or, now that you have light, figure it out the same way we did!* And *There are too many of them, and they're too panicked. They're just going to block the hallway, so Cana and I will never be able to get Enu, Edwy, and Rosi down to Alcibiades before the Enforcers get here. Enu's going to die! Maybe Edwy and Rosi, too!*

Beside me, Cana scrambled toward the top of the rubble. She held the glowing Zacadi pearl up to her mouth. Evidently she'd discovered a secret about the pearl that she hadn't told me: The pearl could also work like a megaphone. Her little-girl voice soared over all the screams, booming out louder than everyone.

"We know how to escape!" she cried. "You can follow us! But we need your help too! We need three strong people to carry our friends!"

Oh, right, I thought. *Good idea, Cana. Almost.*

I grabbed the pearl from her hands and held it by my own mouth.

"Unless someone helps us, we can't help you!" I cried. "Three strong people! Now! Before the guards come and stop us all!"

The people starting to trickle out of the broken corner of the cage seemed to be fighting one another. I saw one man punch another in the mouth. But moments later, two men and a particularly muscular woman stood before Cana and me.

"Pick up those kids," I told them, pointing back toward Enu, Edwy, and Rosi. "Carry them! And stay right behind us, or else, I swear, I'll let the Enforcers capture you again. . . ."

I saw the three people scoop my brothers and Rosi into strong, powerful arms. In that moment I couldn't have told you what any of those people looked like—whether they had green eyes or brown, whether they had curly hair or straight, whether they had dark skin or light. I wasn't even entirely sure they were two men and a woman. All I cared about was that they held my brothers and Rosi in their arms—easily, effortlessly—and that they were ready to run.

"This way!" I screamed.

Miraculously, we were able to dodge the other people spilling out of the broken cage wall. We had a clear shot to Alcibiades's cage—and to the cure for Enu, Edwy, and Rosi. And there was no sign of any Enforcer guards showing up to investigate the explosion. Not yet, anyway.

Cana tugged on my arm.

"Those people are still trapped," she told me, pointing to the opposite side of the prison. I saw that some of the rubble from the explosion had blocked the gap in their bars. "They need help too."

I touched the remaining Zacadi pearls in my pocket. I'd used two to blow up the door. I still needed to blast Alcibiades out of his cage, and to blast a route from the prison to the spaceship that Alcibiades claimed was parked nearby. Then we needed pearls to fuel our flight to the intergalactic court. I'd already started with fewer Zacadi pearls than Alcibiades had told me to bring.

"We'll help those people later," I lied to Cana. "After we get help for Enu, Edwy, and Rosi."

Cana shot one more glance toward the cages on our left. People shoved their arms out through the bars to reach for us; they begged, "Help us! Help us! We're innocent humans like you. . . ."

"We're coming back!" Cana called to them. "I promise!"

I just made a little girl lie . . . , I thought.

But there was no time to feel guilty. Panic and fear carried me along. We passed the last cage full of humans, turned the corner, and reached the edge of the cage full of the dying Zacadians. All I could see were lumps of bodies.

Cana grabbed the translator from the wall, but I didn't wait to make sure she'd turned it on.

"Alcibiades! Hurry! Please—"

I couldn't put the right words together, couldn't explain how desperately Enu, Edwy, and Rosi needed help right *now*.

One of the lumps rose toward us. My eyes made out tentacles. Behind me, the calls for rescue turned into screams of terror. People fell to the ground in a panic.

"*These* aliens are on our side," I snapped. "Now— everyone—stand back!"

I didn't have time to make sure that anyone obeyed. I put a Zacadi pearl on the floor beside the door of Alcibiades's cage. Out of the corner of my eye I saw one of the men—the one carrying Edwy?—reach for it.

"You fool! I said, stand back!" I screamed.

With one hand I shoved back against that man's chest. With the other, I hurled a second Zacadi pearl at the one on the floor.

I missed.

CHAPTER THIRTY-FIVE

The Zacadi pearl I'd thrown hit the floor with a burst of light and a pop that sounded like a dud firecracker sizzling out without exploding. It was a good five centimeters away from the Zacadi pearl it was supposed to hit.

"Will it work if I throw it again?" I screamed at Alcibiades.

I couldn't hear his answer; I couldn't even tell if he tried to answer. My ears had started working strangely, going long moments without hearing anything, even as humans screamed behind me and the cageful of Zacadians grunted and moaned.

Maybe I was about to pass out.

Someone tugged on my arm.

Cana.

" . . . enough that we can shove Rosi, Edwy, and Enu through," she said.

She let go of my arm and began yanking on one bar of the Zacadians' cage. Strangely, it seemed to bend. Cana was practically swinging on it. My eyes tracked her motion, and I understood: She was saying that the force of the one Zacadi pearl hitting the floor had at least cracked that one prison bar, making just enough room for us to push my brothers and Rosi into the Zacadians' cage to be cured.

"Do it!" I screamed. "What she said!"

Maybe nobody could tell that I was about to faint. Maybe they actually believed that I knew what I was saying.

Or maybe they all just trusted Cana. The three strong human escapees holding Edwy, Enu, and Rosi began shoving the flopping, unconscious bodies of my brothers and friend into the Zacadians' cage. I saw the broken, jagged edge of the bar scrape Enu's arm. Blood dripped to the floor.

What if I'm wrong about everything? I thought. *What if the Zacadians don't want to help us, but, but . . .*

Enu, Edwy, and Rosi seemed to be swallowed up in the vast, slimy, tentacled mass of Zacadians.

"What's happening?" I cried. "What are you doing?"

A tentacle reached through the bars and pulled me toward the cage as well. I heard groans and grunts and slurps. I dug my heel into the floor.

And then Cana waved the translator toward my ear. I heard Alcibiades's voice—or, rather, the mechanical voice translating Alcibiades's Zacadian language into something I could understand: "Hurry! We need the other Zacadi pearls!"

I reached for the unexploded Zacadi pearl I'd placed on the floor. But a tentacle swiped it away before I could get my fingers around it.

"Let me—" I began.

"Don't you see the Enforcers coming? We have to go *now*!" Alcibiades screamed at me. Or, at least, the translator did.

I glanced back over my shoulder. There was an unearthly glow behind me, back where I'd exploded the door. I heard a mechanical voice repeat again and again, "Return to your prison cells and nobody will be hurt. Return to your prison cells and nobody will be hurt. Otherwise, we will start crowd-control retaliation in five minutes . . . in four minutes and fifty seconds . . . in four minutes and forty seconds . . ."

The crowd of escapees screamed. Some began scurrying back toward their cells. Other ran in the opposite direction.

Alcibiades yanked Cana and me through the bars of his prison cell. I felt a searing pain in my side. I looked down and saw my own blood dripping toward the floor.

I slammed my hand over the pocketful of Zacadi pearls, protecting them.

"Enu, Edwy, and Rosi have to be ready to go with us," I cried.

I saw Edwy and Rosi sit up dazedly from the mass of lumpy, slimy Zacadians.

"What—what's going on?" Edwy sputtered.

I grabbed his arm, pulling him toward me.

"No time to explain," I called. "Just—"

I felt a tentacle knock my arm to the side and slither into my pocket. No—a hand. Cana's hand.

"Don't worry, Alcibiades," she cried. "I remember where you said to put it."

Cana pulled one of the Zacadi pearls from my pocket and began running toward the wall at the opposite side of the cell. She stood on tiptoes and wedged the pearl into a little hollow that seemed about as high as she could possibly reach. All the Zacadians began rolling away from that wall. Out of the corner of my eye, I saw Alcibiades rear back one of his tentacles, as if he was about to throw the pearl at the wall.

As fast as I could, I grabbed his tentacles.

"You wait until that little girl gets back here with us!" I screamed at him.

He shook his tentacle out of my grasp just as Cana turned and ran back toward us. Cana dove for the lumpy pile of Zacadians. Alcibiades's tentacle flapped back and forward. I couldn't tell whether he released the pearl or not.

But a second later the whole world seemed to explode.

CHAPTER
THIRTY-SIX

The force of the blast threw me backward. I'd worried about Cana, but *I* was actually closer to the wall and the explosion than she was when the pearls collided.

I landed hard, my limbs sprawled in all directions. I heard an unintelligible roar and then a muffled "Run!" coming from the translator that Cana still held as she crawled from the pile of Zacadians.

"Where? Wait—are we all—"

I wanted a moment to think, to assess the situation and plan ahead. But the floor was moving beneath me. No— it was waves of Zacadians moving beneath me, struggling toward a broken place that appeared in the wall as the dust began to settle.

I righted myself, pulled myself to my feet.

"Enu? Edwy? Rosi?" I called.

"Right here," Edwy answered, from just behind me.

I turned my head and saw he was holding up a fist—or,

not quite a fist. It was just his hand, with his fingers entwined with Rosi's. He and Rosi were holding hands.

My mind thought there was actually time to sputter out, *Aw, how sweet*, before my mouth took over, barking out, "Can you walk? Or run? We've got to get out of here!"

"I could run a marathon," Edwy boasted, scrambling to his feet. He swayed unsteadily, and his face still had a sickly tint to it—he looked more likely to vomit than to run. But if he had his bravado back, then he was good to go. At least as ready as I was, anyway.

We were true Watanabonesets. Which reminded me . . .

"Enu? Enu? Where are you?"

Somehow in the din of all the Zacadian groans and the human screams and the Enforcer shouts growing closer and closer, I could still make out one particular grunt coming from a pile of Zacadians. Frantically, I shoved away tentacles, and there was Enu, blinking slowly up at me.

"S-sis?" he managed to whisper.

I grabbed him by the arms, but of course I wasn't strong enough to lift him. I nudged his torso toward Alcibiades.

"*You* have to carry Enu," I screamed. "He's too weak to run right now, and you're the only one with muscles—or, well, whatever Zacadians have instead of muscles!"

Alcibiades scooped up Enu, but the motion seemed like an afterthought—just a way to get Enu's body out of his way.

"Unless Enu ends up on that spaceship with us, I'm throwing all the Zacadi pearls out the window!" I threatened.

I don't know if Alcibiades heard me—there were still too many screams and shouts and moans and grunts echoing all around us. And the walls still might have been reverberating with the aftershocks from the explosion. But Alcibiades tightened his grip on Enu's body and brought a second tentacle forward to draw him close. I decided Enu was safe enough—for now—and I grabbed Edwy's available hand and pulled him and Rosi along with me. Rosi, I saw, clutched Cana's hand as well.

The six of us surged forward, struggling toward the opening in the wall. Pale light shone in through the hole—was it moonlight? Had Alcibiades really blasted a new exit to the outside?

Would it be worth anything if we immediately met a cluster of Enforcers once we surfaced?

"Hurry!" I screamed at the others. "We have to be fast. . . ."

Alcibiades was screaming the same thing. Then my ears blanked out again for a moment, and I felt like I was in one of those dreams where you run and run and run and try your very hardest, but you don't make any progress at all. There were too many Zacadians in our way, too many humans reaching toward the hole in the wall or trying to crawl toward it by squeezing under the gap I'd created in the prison bars.

Alcibiades grunted something beside me, and a moment later I heard the translator in Cana's hand scream out, "I promise!" And then everything changed. The Zacadians around us seemed to be shoving us forward, lifting us toward the hole in the wall, even as they rose up and blocked the stream of humans struggling toward the hole themselves. In seconds my knees met rock, and I started climbing and climbing and climbing. And then I popped my head up into fresh air and shadowy moonlight.

Oddly, there seemed to be two sets of shadows creeping toward me from two different directions.

Oh, right, this planet has two moons, which means two light sources to cast shadows.

Off to my left, a long, straight silhouette stood silent and motionless in the night sky, framed by a half-risen moon.

The spaceship, I told myself, breathing a sigh of relief. *And it's not even that far away.*

To the right, the shadows were jumbled, constantly shifting. Fearfully, I forced my eyes to follow the shadows to their source: figures also framed by a rising moon, but not still or silent. These shapes were chaotic and loud and streaming toward us.

These were Enforcers. Holding guns.

CHAPTER
THIRTY-SEVEN

"Go! Go! Go! Go!" I screamed, even as I scrambled out of the hole and yanked Edwy and Rosi up behind me. "Cana, hide your light! All of you—stay low, and maybe they won't see us—maybe they can't shoot—"

Already I could see the flaw in my thinking. I was screaming about the wrong danger. Why would the Enforcers shoot when they had the power to take over our bodies and make us do anything they wanted? This was hopeless.

My body didn't seem to know that. I kept reaching down into the hole, kept tugging on arms and legs and hands and feet. I wasn't going to give up until I had to. Edwy, Rosi, and Cana joined me crouched in the rubble at the edge of the hole, reaching down for Enu and Alcibiades behind us.

"Are there Enforcers surrounding the spaceship?" Alcibiades gasped at me. At least, the voice coming out of the translator seemed to be gasping.

I risked a quick, darting glance over my shoulder toward the spaceship.

"No, all the Enforcers are on the other side of us," I hissed back to him. "Coming from where we were always sent out to work—do they have barracks there?" What good were my descriptions, when he'd never seen my brothers and friends and me being sent out to work?

Alcibiades grunted and panted, but the translator didn't supply any words for his sounds. Maybe his strength was flagging; maybe he'd gone nonverbal on me. The Zacadians below him made panicky moans and groans, and the translator evidently judged that worth decoding. I heard a jumbled "Plan B, then?" "Do we have to?" "It is better to die with valor and for a cause . . ."

"Um, did someone say 'die'?" I asked, my voice shaking with fear. "Can't we stop and think and maybe—"

Alcibiades slithered out of the hole, his last tentacle erupting from the small space with a *pop!* In one motion he scooped up Edwy, Rosi, Cana, and me alongside Enu. I'd never gotten a good count of how many tentacles Alcibiades had, so maybe he could have clutched us with one tentacle apiece. But I found myself upside down and face-to-face with Enu, our foreheads pressed tightly together as Alcibiades slid toward the spaceship.

"Are you okay?" I whispered to Enu. "Feeling any better?"

Even in the moonlight I could see the angry flush to Enu's face. He rolled his head to the side, and we were squeezed so closely together that his motion rolled my head to the side as well. Now I was staring straight at the Enforcers running toward us.

"Who cares if I'm still sick or not?" Enu hissed. "That monster's using us like a shield, blocking the Enforcers from shooting *him*. We're all going to die!"

Was Enu right?

It felt like we were in a video game, with the Enforcers running after us, carrying guns. Every video game Enu played was set up this way, with good guys fighting enemies. Sometimes there were two sets of enemies, and that made things even trickier.

Enu had played a lot more video games than I ever had. Was he right, that both the Enforcers and Alcibiades were our enemies?

I started trying to squirm away from Alcibiades.

He roared at me then. "No! You have to help!" came grunting out of the translator, which Cana evidently still carried in her hand. Another roar, and then "As long as we're all pressed together, that confuses their weapons, and they can't take control of our bodies!"

Okay, then, I thought, and stopped squirming.

"But their bullets can still hit our bodies, right?" Enu

argued. "Bullets don't care what a body's made of. . . ."

Alcibiades and the translator stayed silent.

Right now Alcibiades's life counts for more than any of us humans, I thought. *He knows how to fly that spaceship. We don't. Maybe he does need us as shields.*

The thought froze me in place. Alcibiades kept slinking forward.

Behind us the Enforcers were gaining ground. They were just a few meters back from the hole we'd crawled from. Two or three of the ones at the very front raised guns to their shoulders. I cowered and winced, so I could only see through the slits of my eyelids.

But then tentacles began spilling out of the hole in the ground: One Zacadian after another began slithering out and shakily standing upright.

"No, no—it's dangerous out here! You all need to stay safe!" Rosi screamed back at them, just as Enu screamed, "Stop! Stay back! There's not room on the spaceship for everyone!"

Two different viewpoints. Two different reactions.

Was this the true difference between being raised in a Fredtown and on Earth?

I didn't know what to say or do. That was an Earth reaction too.

One of the Zacadians who had emerged from the hole

fell to the ground, and another instantly popped up to take its place.

I jerked on Enu's arm.

"They're protecting us!" I screamed in his ear. "They aren't coming up to get on the ship! They're sacrificing themselves so *we* can escape!"

"Are you sure?" Enu asked, as if this was too incredible to believe. He struggled against Alcibiades's grip, lifting his head and chest so he could see better.

Something went zinging over my head. A bullet.

"That was close," I whispered to Enu, but something was wrong. He didn't answer. His body slumped suddenly, his head thudding against mine. Even in the unbelievable Zacadi overnight chill, I felt a warm trickle against my arm.

Enu had been shot.

CHAPTER THIRTY-EIGHT

"Help! Stop! We have to—Enu—"

I couldn't gather the words to explain what I'd seen, what I was struggling to understand. I felt an arm on my neck—Rosi pulling my head down so *I* wouldn't be hit too.

"Why didn't you do that for Enu?" I snarled, though maybe what I really meant was, *Why didn't I do that for Enu?*

I sobbed into Alcibiades's slimy back. The wind whistled through my hair.

"First aid!" Edwy screamed in my ear. "Do you know first aid? Does anyone?"

"Apply pressure on the wound!" Rosi screamed. "Stop the bleeding!"

I turned my head, and I saw that *she* couldn't reach Enu; only I could.

"I'm only good at computers," I muttered. "Computers and technology and . . ."

Edwy shoved my elbow, and my hands pressed into the blood.

The wound was on Enu's shoulder, not his head.

Even I knew shoulder wounds were survivable. They could be.

I pressed my hands as hard as I could against Enu's shoulder as Alcibiades kept rushing forward, jolting us over the barren landscape. I could hear the gunfire behind us; I could hear the screams and shouts of the Enforcers and the groans and wails of the falling Zacadians.

And then Alcibiades slammed against hard metal, opened a door. He grabbed the Zacadi pearl Cana was hiding— the one we'd been using for light—and shoved it into a slot above the door. I heard a hum: The spaceship was powering up, coming back to life. Cana, Rosi, and Edwy scrambled upward, along a ladder that fell before us from a metal cylinder. I tugged on Enu's blood-soaked shirt.

"You'll have to carry him!" I screamed at Alcibiades. "Enu needs help!"

Maybe the translator made my words intelligible to Alcibiades; maybe he spat back a reply. I didn't hear any of it.

"Get out of the way!" I screamed at Cana, Rosi, and Edwy, because they were all reaching down, all trying to grasp Enu's limp body. And they were all so small; they were accomplishing nothing but putting themselves in danger too.

Maybe my mind blanked out a little, because suddenly we were all rising—oh, Alcibiades had hit some lever that carried the ladder up into the spaceship with us on it. The door shut below us—were we finally safe?

The six of us lay in a pile on some metal floor.

"Enu," I said, shaking my brother's shoulder. "Enu, wake up. Someone has to take care of you—"

"The pearls!" Alcibiades screamed at me, the sound coming from the translator and his mouth almost simultaneously. "We have to have the rest of your Zacadi pearls to get us out of here! Both of them! Now!"

"Oh, but I only have one left," I said, patting my pocket. I was momentarily confused that Alcibiades didn't know this.

Oh, right, it wasn't like there was time to explain that I couldn't steal all the pearls we needed . . . not when my brothers and Rosi had to be cured and there were all those other prisoners begging for help and then the Enforcers were chasing us. . . .

"We wouldn't have any left if I hadn't missed with that one throw," I tried to explain. "So maybe . . ."

There was no point in continuing to talk. I hadn't figured out Alcibiades's features exactly, but my best guess was that his expression now would translate into a human face with eyes widened with extreme horror.

He roared so loudly I had to cover my ears. But the translator's voice broke through anyway:

"Then we don't have enough fuel to take off!" it wailed at me. "We can't go anywhere!"

CHAPTER
THIRTY-NINE

Two things happened at once: I heard a pinging beneath us that might have been the Enforcers' bullets hitting the side of the spaceship.

And Cana pressed the translator into Alcibiades's tentacles.

"Didn't you say there's a pearl inside that makes this work?" she asked.

Alcibiades's eyes widened again. He grabbed the translator and smashed it against the floor. With one tentacle, he scooped something from the wreckage—a pearl. Another tentacle slithered toward me.

I already had my pearl out of my pocket, held out to him.

Alcibiades grabbed the pearl from my hand. Then he slammed both pearls into a compartment high over our heads, higher than any of us humans could have reached. A control panel rose out of the floor, and Alcibiades began running tentacles across the screen, his motions so smooth and fast that my vision blurred.

Or maybe the blurring effect was from the spaceship lifting so *rapidly*, spinning up and up and up.

I stopped hearing any bullets hitting the spaceship.

And Alcibiades said that's all the Enforcers have to attack us with here on Zacadi; once we're in space we'll be out of range. . . .

I hoped Alcibiades was right.

We all began to float.

"This is much better than the way we left Fredtown," Edwy called as he bounced gently off the ceiling.

"Or Earth!" Rosi reminded him.

Both their voices were full of fake cheer, like they were trying hard to stay hopeful.

Then Cana added, "We'll be able to get help for Enu really soon, Kiandra," and I had to choke back sobs.

Enu was floating away from me. Little droplets of blood spun around him in a horrifying dance.

Would blood even clot in space? I wondered. *Or do wounds just bleed and bleed and . . .*

"How soon?" I snapped at Alcibiades. "How long will it take to get to the planet where the intergalactic court meets? Or—any other planet where Enu could get help?"

Alcibiades kept his head bent over the control panel, his tentacles flying. I grabbed one of them and asked my question again.

Now Alcibiades looked up, nothing but puzzlement on his face.

Right. Without the translator, he didn't understand.

"Cana, did you learn enough of the Zacadian language that *you* can be our interpreter?" Rosi asked, tapping the younger girl on the shoulder as she floated by. "Can you ask Alcibiades how soon we can get Enu to a doctor?"

"I'll *try*," Cana said.

Painstakingly, she began to moan and grunt. The sounds went on and on, indecipherable. Alcibiades seemed to be trying to listen, but then he only shrugged helplessly, gave a single grunt, and turned back to the control panel, which he held on to with a single tentacle.

"What did he say?" I asked.

Cana bit her lip.

"I think that was, 'I'm doing the best I can,'" she reported. "But I could be wrong."

I reached for Enu, but he was too far away.

"Isn't there a way to create fake gravity on a spaceship?" I asked desperately. "A way to tie Enu to the wall so he won't keep floating—and bleeding? A way to . . . to know that everything is going to be all right?"

"Everything *is* going to be all right," Rosi said quickly. "We'll figure out a way to talk to Alcibiades without the translator. He'll help us figure out how to help Enu. He'll be fine. You'll see."

But I couldn't believe a word she said, because she'd been raised by Freds.

And Alcibiades was a totally alien creature.

And Enu, my brother Enu, who'd been with me for my entire life, was just as likely to die as he was to live.

CHAPTER FORTY

For a long time I was worthless. Rosi was the one who snagged Enu by the foot and pulled him over to one wall, strapping him in somehow to hold him in one place. Edwy took his shirt off and tore it into strips, then tied the strips around Enu's shoulder as makeshift bandages. Cana found a blanket somewhere and tucked it around Enu.

"Now he can sleep while we fly," she announced. "My Fred-mommy always said sleep is good when you're sick or hurt."

Then the three younger kids began using other blankets to corral all the blood droplets into one section of the ship— its toilet, maybe? The Zacadian equivalent of a toilet?

"Want to race for the ones over there?" Edwy called to Rosi and Cana. He pointed toward the droplets that had floated the farthest away.

Is this just a game to you? I wanted to scream at them. *Don't you understand? Enu could die! All of us could die!*

Maybe Edwy was just trying to keep Cana from seeing what serious danger we were in. Maybe that was something he'd learned from the Freds. But that made me mad too. The Freds had never understood Enu or me. Being raised by Freds meant Edwy, Rosi, and Cana couldn't fully understand either.

Enu would understand everything, if he ever woke up again. He and I understood each other; we'd always been alike. It had always been just the two of us against the world— the two of us against our parents, the two of us against nasty nannies and the indifferent school, the two of us against Udans.

Udans . . .

I gasped, because I hadn't thought about Udans in days. We'd left him behind on Earth in danger, protecting *us*, and I'd all but forgotten him.

Maybe Rosi forgot Bobo, too, and Edwy forgot Zeba. . . .

No, right this minute Rosi was floating past me, calling back over her shoulder as her hair bushed out from her head, "You know, if Bobo were here, he would *love* helping catch all the blood. He'd have a million questions about zero gravity and if the blood looks like this inside our bodies, too. . . ."

I kicked off against a ridge on the wall that had undoubtedly been designed for creatures with tentacles, not hands and feet. That floated me back toward Alcibiades. I wrapped my leg around the post holding up the control panel so I didn't just bounce backward. Alcibiades was no longer flailing his tentacles about wildly; now he was just staring at the screen filled with indecipherable symbols.

When I touched the frame of the control panel, reddish dirt came off on my hand—I guess the spaceship had been abandoned for so long that this layer of dust had grown into a hardened casing. But the dirt gave me an idea.

Painstakingly, I used my finger to draw two circles in the dust. I added an arcing line between them, and a question mark over the line. I hoped Alcibiades would understand that I was asking, *How long before we get to the planet of the intergalactic court?*

To help out, I drew another circle off to the side, with arrows around it to show it spinning. Then I wrote beside that:

1?

2?

3?

Wouldn't Alcibiades understand that I was showing his planet making a complete rotation, that I was asking about the number of days we had to travel?

Alcibiades stared helplessly; then a wave of motion shivered through his whole body. It seemed like a shrug.

Of course. Why would Alcibiades understand my symbol

for a question mark? Or for numbers? Or even arrows?

Alcibiades and I were from different planets. We were different *species*. Just because the translator had made it seem like we could communicate easily before, that didn't actually mean anything. For all I knew, maybe he wasn't even taking us to the intergalactic court.

And yet, when I stared into his eyes—which had finally stopped rolling up and down—I felt like we *did* understand each other.

Both of us were scared.

And both of us still had hope that everything would work out.

CHAPTER
FORTY-ONE

When you're not on a planet, there's no such thing as day or night. I felt like I'd lost seconds, minutes, and hours, too. We had times of sleeping and times of waking. We had times of checking on Enu, and nothing to comfort us but the proof that he was still drawing shallow breaths, in and out. He was still alive.

Beyond that, the only thing we had to measure time was our growing hunger.

Not long after Rosi, Edwy, and Cana managed to corral the last of the floating blood, Alcibiades let himself sail up from the control panel and reach for a compartment overhead.

It was empty.

Alcibiades let out a distraught roar and clapped a tentacle over his mouth. He gazed despairingly at me, and I understood what he was upset about: He'd expected to find food in that compartment, and there was none. Maybe, as the

Enforcers were taking over Alcibiades's planet and enslaving all his people, some desperate Zacadian had raided this ship for one last meal. Maybe the Enforcers themselves had taken away the food because they didn't want the Zacadians escaping.

"Never mind," I said. "We've been starving for weeks. We can last a little while longer, until we get to the intergalactic court."

Now *I* sounded like someone raised by Freds. I hoped Alcibiades heard the comforting tone in my voice even if he couldn't understand the words.

But the hunger made us dim and vague. Alcibiades knew how to give us water—either there was a tank on board that hadn't been tainted, or the spaceship had some way to recycle the air and pull out hydrogen and oxygen to make liquid. (This occurred to me only after I'd taken many, many sips from a spigot on the wall.) But that left me thinking, *It's only something like three days that people can live without water. It's much longer that people can live without food. But . . . how long? And does it matter that I got food on our last day on Zacadi, but Enu, Edwy, Rosi, and Cana didn't? Does it matter that Enu is wounded and lost a lot of blood? Does that mean he needs food more than the rest of us?*

Does it matter that Alcibiades is a different species and may need food more often than we do? Or . . . less often? Or . . .

I'd fall asleep, wake up, and go back to thinking, *How long can people go without eating? Does Enu need food more because he's injured? Does Alcibiades, because he's a foreign species?*

We stopped talking much to one another, because what was there to say?

I wanted to apologize to Alcibiades for not doing anything while his fellow Zacadians bravely stood between us and the Enforcers—while the Zacadians died for *us*. I wanted to apologize to Cana for turning her into a liar, letting her assure the other human prisoners that we'd come back for them, that we'd rescue them, too.

But what did that matter, when the six of us who'd made it to the spaceship were probably going to die too?

Strangely, I began thinking more and more of my parents. When their hometown had exploded in war, they'd thought only of saving their own children. They hadn't tried to help anyone else, unless I counted Udans, their employee. (*Did* I count Udans? Did they?) I understood my parents better now. Escaping from prison, I'd thought only of rescuing my brothers and friends. I'd lied to convince other people to help us, and then I'd abandoned them completely. What my parents had done was cruel; what I'd done was cruel. They'd been in an unbearable, unwinnable situation, and so had I.

But there's still hope for me; there's still time. Isn't there? If we make it to the intergalactic court, we can get help for every-one we left behind—if anyone's still alive.

Wasn't there still hope?

I couldn't talk about this with anyone else, because I might say there wasn't hope. I couldn't do that to Edwy, Rosi, and Cana.

So I communicated with the three of them mainly by grunting, just as I did with Alcibiades. After a while, maybe I even started to lose the ability to *think* in anything but grunts, because my thoughts became even more disjointed, more like *Food . . . water . . . Enu . . . Alcibiades . . . help . . . parents . . . forgive . . . help . . .*

And then one morning (afternoon? Evening? Night? Who knew?) I suddenly heard a booming voice fill the space-ship with a roar and grunts and groans and moans.

"Is that . . . a Zacadian talking to us?" I asked weakly, barely able to lift my head to listen. "We've traveled all this time and we're still close enough to Zacadi that communications come in that way?"

"Maybe it's just . . . prerecorded," Edwy groaned to me as he floated vacantly past.

It took me a minute to understand—he thought it was just a voice that went along with the ship. Maybe one of us had accidently jarred a lever that triggered a routine, auto-matic response.

But Alcibiades didn't react as though what we were hearing were automatic or routine. He'd been floating above me, his tentacles streaming listlessly around him in a way that made him appear more than ever like a jellyfish. But now he suddenly jerked to attention. He shot a tentacle out and shoved off against the area I thought of as the ceiling of our compartment (though of course there really was no up or down anymore.) That zipped him over to the control panel, and he began flapping tentacles across the screen just as urgently as he'd done when we were blasting off.

"Ah—oog—an—oo!" he screamed, and somehow it occurred to me that he might be saying something like "Don't shoot!"

I shoved off the wall and flailed toward him.

"Please! Help us! We're in desperate need! One of us is injured!" I shouted, just in case whoever we were talking to would be friendlier to humans than Zacadians.

The voice roared back, a tidal wave of grunts and groans. And then, surprisingly, it switched to the language I could understand, even though the words came out oddly accented:

"We repeat: You are in intergalactic-court territory now. No one is allowed to enter or leave without permission. Your incursion into this zone will be treated as an enemy attack unless you explain your presence instantly. Countdown to destruction begins now. . . ."

CHAPTER
FORTY-TWO

I don't know what Alcibiades said, but I could hear him groaning and moaning as I screamed, "We're five innocent humans and one innocent Zacadian! Our only crime was to exist! Ask the Enforcers why we had to escape to here! And . . . ask the Freds! They care a lot about three of the children on our ship, even if they don't care about the rest of us!"

Silence from the voice. I could hear only Cana squeaking out, "What's 'destruction' mean?"

She didn't know that word, but evidently she understood enough to react. Tears trembled in her eyelashes.

"There's a little girl on this spaceship who's only *five*!" I screamed, tilting back my head to put more power behind my voice. "That's five in human years, which is almost nothing at all. I don't care what you think about the rest of us, but you can't destroy a child like that—you can't . . . you can't. . . ."

My voice gave out.

It felt like an eternity passed before the mechanical voice

sounded again. It spoke the Zacadian language first, so I had to watch Alcibiades to see if there was any hope. Shivers rolled through his body, but were they hopeful or despairing?

Finally I heard the language I could understand:

"We will let you land. We will take you into observational quarantine."

"Thank you—but my brother will need medical treatment right away!" I answered. "And we all need food!"

Alcibiades gave a long moan—was he making a different request? Asking for directions?

Then, suddenly, at the end of his moan I no longer heard it as a moan. I heard words that made sense.

"As I said, I can land more easily if I have the ability to communicate with my shipmates." The words seemed to come straight out of Alcibiades's mouth.

I clutched one of his tentacles.

"What did you just ask for?" I cried. "To be granted—"

"Alcibiades! We can understand you perfectly again!" Cana squealed.

He stared at Cana and me in wonder.

"They made it so you learned my Zacadian language?" he asked in astonishment. "They could implant that in your brain even from so far away?"

"No, they just made you speak human." I shook my head. "How can you do that?"

Rosi tapped me on the shoulder.

"I think he's hearing us in his language and we're hearing him in ours," she said, and actually laughed. "Isn't this great? I think I'm going to like the intergalactic court!"

"Especially if they have ice cream sundaes," Edwy said in a croak. I realized it had been a long time since I'd heard him speak. But he quickly sounded like himself again. "Ice cream sundaes and cookies and cakes and puddings . . . yikes, even *spinach* sounds good to me right now!"

We were all as giddy as Edwy as we prepared to land—well, we all were except for Enu. I went over and grabbed his hand and whispered, "We made it! Someone who knows what they're doing can help you now!"

His hand was still warm. His pulse still throbbed weakly beneath his skin. He was going to be okay.

"I thought this moment would never come," Alcibiades marveled as he hunched over the control panel. "I was writing our story in the ship's computer system, so whoever found us would know. . . . Now we can tell our story directly to the intergalactic court."

"To *Freds* on the intergalactic court," Cana said.

My eyes met Edwy's and Rosi's, over Cana's head. Edwy stopped crowing about cookies and cakes.

"At least we had enough fuel to get here after all," I said, not willing to let go of our gleeful moment.

"We had enough to get here going super slow," Alcibiades said. "We would have been here in five minutes, not five days, if we'd had that other Zacadi pearl."

Five days. That was how long we'd gone without food. No wonder I felt faint.

That was also how long Enu had gone without medical treatment.

"But we made it," Rosi said firmly. "Did you know Kiandra managed to get every single one of the Zacadi pearls herself?"

"I owe you my life," Alcibiades said, in a deeply resonant voice that sounded nothing like his Zacadian grunts and groans or the translator's robotic tone. It didn't fit at all coming from a creature that looked like a mutant cross between a slug, an octopus, and an oversize jellyfish.

"We owe you *our* lives," I muttered, embarrassed. A vision rose up in my mind of our frantic fleeing: Alcibiades carrying us, his fellow Zacadians streaming out of the prison and falling before the Enforcers' gunfire . . . "We owe you and all the other Zacadians who . . . who . . ."

Before I could say more, the booming voice came back: "We have you locked into our guidance system, overriding your controls. Please strap yourselves in for landing."

"Hey, we did okay floating around during takeoff!" Edwy joked.

"That's because Alcibiades was flying us then," Cana said, blinking up adoringly at the tentacled creature.

"Wouldn't seat belts be a little more important during a landing?" Rosi asked. "Because we're hitting the ground? And returning to gravity?"

"What you would call 'seat belts' in this spaceship are designed to be wrapped around tentacles, but here, I'll help you adapt," Alcibiades said.

He started by tying Enu in more securely, then reached out tentacles to help the rest of us.

Nine. I finally counted his tentacles, and that was how many he had.

We glided smoothly down to the ground, and I began to feel an odd, unfamiliar tugging on my body. Was the gravity of the intergalactic court's planet even more intense than gravity on Zacadi, or was I just unaccustomed to any gravity after five days in outer space?

I felt light-headed, as though all the blood in my body was rushing toward my feet.

Why hadn't Alcibiades told us to strap in upside down?

Because what would he understand about human bodies? I reminded myself.

Our spaceship descended faster and faster. The forces acting on my body pulled my eyes into slits and drew the skin of my face back toward my ears. I stopped being able to see or hear.

230

And then everything was still. We stopped moving.

"Help my brother first," I moaned, as soon as I could string words together again. My vision was still spotty. My hearing, too—I couldn't really tell if Alcibiades, Edwy, Rosi, and Cana were calling out similar pleas. I couldn't see how Enu was doing. But I dizzily lifted my head from the padded wall behind me and raised my voice, as if that would make the authorities of the intergalactic court hear me better. "He's injured, and the landing might have reopened his wounds, and . . ."

And then people in uniforms were streaming onto the spaceship. I saw them only in flashes, barely distinct as I tried to blink my vision back to normalcy. So it took me a moment to realize:

They all looked human. Completely human.

"You're . . . you're from Earth?" I gasped, as a woman untied me from the wall. "Like us? The intergalactic court hired humans to serve as medics?"

"Of course not," the man behind her practically snarled. "You're in intergalactic court territory. The protocols apply, even in the docking port area."

"The . . . protocols?" I repeated stupidly.

"Everybody here sees everybody else as being a member of his or her own species," the woman said. "No matter what anyone really is. It's like how you can hear your own language, even though I'm speaking mine."

I'd known that odd detail about the intergalactic court. Supposedly, that made everyone understand each other better, to see everybody on the court as the same. I remembered telling Edwy that information way back on Earth, and acting like he was an idiot for not knowing.

"But . . . what are you *really*?" I asked. "What planet are you from?"

"Want to see?" the man taunted. He ran his fingers over my eyelids. When I opened my eyes again, the human faces of the man and woman before me had melted away, revealing hard, scaly beetlelike heads.

"Nooo . . . ," I moaned.

Frantically I looked past the man and woman bent over me, to the other uniformed creatures flooding onto the spaceship.

Every single one of them was an Enforcer.

CHAPTER
FORTY-THREE

"**No, no, no, no—**" My vision slipped back into seeing the man and woman beside me as human, but I shoved their hands away. "You can't—this isn't fair. We can't plead our case to *Enforcers*. You have to—"

"But it's Enforcers who meet all unauthorized visitors," the man growled. "That's the setup."

"Then send us to your diplomats," I begged. "Give us a fair hearing. Please—"

"I think this counts as recalcitrant behavior, don't you?" the woman muttered to the man.

The man nodded, and I felt a prick against my arm. And then everything went black.

When I woke up again, I was in a dark, shadowy room. The ceiling above me arced in an oddly familiar way, and I automatically reached out my left arm as though I knew a bedside light was going to be right there.

It was. I pressed a button, and I was surrounded by a

warm glow illuminating a familiar bedside table and a familiar jumble of electronic devices and cords. And beyond it, a familiar room with rainbow bottles of nail polish on the dresser and shorts and T-shirts strewn about the floor.

It appeared that I was back on Earth, back in Refuge City, back in my ordinary bedroom. The only clue that I hadn't just dreamed the past five days—or the past five weeks—was a tender bruise in the crook of my right elbow, the kind of bruise left behind by an IV.

"*What* is going on?" I demanded. "Enu? Edwy? Are you—"

My door cracked open almost instantly. But it wasn't either of my brothers who appeared in the doorway. It was a gray-haired old woman with a soft, kind human face.

"This is more trickery, right?" I snarled at her. "You're fooling me again, making me think I'm back home. These mind games—do you think you're going to break me? Are you really an Enforcer too?"

"An Enforcer? No, of course not," the woman said, distress flowing over her gentle features. "Don't you like your special room?"

I shook my head hard, which sent jagged bolts of pain searing through my body. The woman patted my face, which somehow took the pain away.

"Be still, be at peace," she murmured.

"Not when even the room around me is a *lie*," I protested.

The woman's gentle eyes actually held tears of sympathy now.

"Oh dear, I'm so sorry you feel that way," she began. It was hard not to believe she was sincere. "We thought the familiar scene would be comforting. We went to great trouble with the authenticity. We had images specially beamed from Earth for you. But maybe humans raised on Earth aren't . . . Oh, never mind. Is this better?"

She pressed something on the wall, and the electronic devices, the nail polish, and the jumble of clothes disappeared. So did the arched ceiling. Suddenly I appeared to be in a sterile hospital room.

"Yes, it *is* better," I said. "Because this is *really* what I'm surrounded by. Right?"

The woman nodded. I looked down at the long tunic I was wearing, which seemed to be wavering between looking like a hospital gown and my favorite T-shirt from home—a slouchy purple jersey with a ripped pocket.

"And my real clothes are . . . ?" I began.

The woman sighed.

"You're still wearing the clothes you arrived in," she said. The hazy look around my shirt disappeared, and I saw the blue T-shirt and khaki shorts I'd been wearing since I left Earth. Somehow they seemed cleaner and newer.

"Of course we disinfected and reconditioned them," the woman said. "Your medical condition didn't require anything else. But if you want to change, we could—"

I reached for the back pocket of my shorts. My phone was still there. I wanted to look at it—to see if maybe when they were reconditioning my clothes, they'd recharged my phone. But I didn't want the woman to see me do that.

"I'm good," I said.

The woman still wore an expression of deep concern.

"You've clearly been through a lot," she murmured comfortingly. "Our intentions with all those changes truly were to help you heal. Psychologically. Spiritually. We find that typically more of a homey touch works wonders. . . ."

"I'm not typical, okay?"

The woman's face softened with even more apologetic sympathy, but I regarded her with suspicion. I wanted to ask about the others—especially Enu—but I didn't trust her yet.

I didn't want her to know I had any weaknesses.

"If you aren't really a human or an Enforcer, what are you?" I asked.

"Usually people can tell right away . . . ," she murmured. "Of course I'm a Fred. A healer Fred. Many of us do go into the healing professions. . . ."

I'd always told myself that if I ever met a Fred, I'd punch first and ask questions later. But there was a sincerity about this woman I hadn't expected. A . . . simpleness.

But maybe that was just more of the illusion.

"Show me," I snarled. "Let me see your real face."

"It's really not part of our protocol, but under the circumstances . . . all right," she said.

I wasn't watching her hands, so I couldn't see if she pushed any buttons or levers anywhere. She didn't touch my eyelids like the Enforcer back on the spaceship had. But for an instant I saw a different face behind her human one—a face so kind and good and soft and fuzzy that I wanted to weep and giggle all at once.

And somehow I knew it was completely real.

No wonder that expression could never be captured in video or photos. Everything about it made me forget to analyze it or to count the eyes or debate with myself about whether the exact color of the woman's fur was greenish-blue or more of a bluish-green.

"You're . . . sincere, then?" I asked. "You Freds really do want to help?"

"Of course," the woman said. "Sorrow and pain in any creature breaks our hearts."

Could I actually believe her?

"Then why," I challenged, "do you let the Enforcers—"

Before I could ask the rest of my question, Edwy, Rosi, and Cana bounded into the room.

"You're finally awake!" Rosi cried. "Our Fred-healers promised to call us the minute we were allowed to see you. We've been so worried!"

She didn't look worried anymore. All three of them just looked . . . healthy. Edwy stood tall and proud in new shorts and a large T-shirt that replaced the one he'd torn up for bandages. Could he possibly have grown during the time we were on Zacadi, and I'd never noticed? And Rosi and Cana were no longer the desperate children in tattered clothes that I'd known from the very first, when they were running from Enforcers out in the desert on Earth. Now their eyes glowed from clean faces, and they were wrapped in quilted robes that looked cozy and warm.

I couldn't remember anyone wearing robes like that back on Earth. Maybe just as the healers had tried to comfort me by giving me an imitation of my room back home, Rosi and Cana were being comforted and consoled with clothes from their original homes.

From their Fredtown.

I glanced back at my Fred-healer, who was still gazing compassionately at me, even though she wore a human face again.

Was that how all the adults had always looked at Edwy, Rosi, Cana, and the other kids all the time back in their Fredtown? What was it like to be filled up with that much love and care, from birth on?

I didn't know. It wasn't what Enu and I had had.

Enu . . .

"Have you seen Enu?" I snapped at the younger kids. My voice came out much more harsh than I intended. "Is *he* okay?"

"They say he's healing well, but we can't see him yet," Edwy said. He flicked his gaze toward the Fred-healer and back to me.

That was enough to remind me that he had always hated his Fredtown and resented the Freds who'd raised him.

I slid my legs over the side of the bed and stood up. I tried to pretend the motion didn't make me dizzy yet again.

"Miss! Miss! You aren't fully restored to health yet," the Fred-healer cried. "Please, for your own safety—"

"You say you care about my sorrow and pain?" I asked. "Well, it's only going to get worse until I know my brother's all right."

"I assure you—" the healer began.

"Yeah, well, I come from a place where you can't always believe what adults tell you, so I need to see for myself," I interrupted.

I was so weak she could have held me back just by lightly grasping my arm. I think she could tell that, but she let me slide past.

"He's actually right next door," she murmured. "If peeking in will set your mind at ease, then by all means, I'll allow it."

She followed me out the door, with Edwy, Rosi, and Cana close behind. We turned down a nondescript hallway, and by the time I reached the next door, the healer was in front of me. She gently eased the door open.

"See?" she whispered.

Enu lay propped up and lightly snoring in a hospital bed that could have been the twin of mine. He had been injured badly enough that I was sure they'd thrown his clothes away. The blood-covered strips of Edwy's old T-shirt, which had covered Enu's wounded shoulder for the past five days, were gone, replaced by a small, tidy square of gauze that barely showed above the neckline of his hospital gown.

"Is everything I'm seeing real, or is this another illusion?" I asked. "Is that all you're doing for him? He was shot, and you only gave him one little bandage?"

"She told us they did really, really good surgery," Cana informed me, even as she patted my hand comfortingly. "They know how to put veins and arteries and even capillaries back together. They gave him new blood."

I decided not to ask, *How many bullets did they have to take out?* in front of Cana.

"But he's *still* not awake?" I asked.

"He *was*," the healer admitted. "But he was so agitated, we were afraid he'd injure himself again. We had to give him a sedative."

Agitated? It was like this Fred-woman talked in code.

I shoved the door the rest of the way open and rushed over to Enu's bed.

"Enu, you were ready to tell the intergalactic court what happened, weren't you?" I grabbed his uninjured shoulder and shook it. "Wake up! Remember how you're always telling me that sometimes injured athletes have to play hurt for the sake of their team? Well, now's a time like that. Think of all the prisoners back on Zacadi. Think what the Enforcers might be doing to them while you're snoozing and getting sedatives. Or what might be happening back on Earth. To . . . to . . ."

I couldn't even speak the names of the people I was worried about back on Earth: *Udans. Bobo. Zeba. Our parents . . .*

My shaking got rougher. Enu did nothing but let out a pained groan. The Fred-healer all but flew to my side.

"Young lady, I must insist! You can't disturb another patient like that!" she cried. "Don't you know how severely injured your brother was, and how greatly his life was endangered by the long trip?"

"Yes, I do know," I said. "I was *there*. I could very easily have been shot myself. That's why we need to tell—"

"Don't worry; the younger children already made a full report," the healer said. "I'm sure it will be considered thoroughly. And we can get yours later. Once you've . . . calmed down."

I looked back at Edwy, Rosi, and Cana.

"A man interviewed us," Edwy said grimly.

"He was nice," Cana offered. "But he kept saying we shouldn't be scared. Don't you think it was right to be scared, when we were running away and people were being shot?"

"Has the intergalactic court taken any action because of that report?" I asked the healer.

"Oh, I can't keep track of the court's every decision, for every sector of the universe," she said apologetically. "They'll do what's right. I trust them to take wise action when they need to."

"*I* don't," I said. I pointed toward my chest. "Trust issues, remember?"

To my surprise, Rosi stepped up behind me, backing me up. It was almost like she was threatening the healer.

"We *all* need to know what the intergalactic court has been doing about the Enforcers on Zacadi and on Earth—and probably other places as well," she said.

"I need to know too," a voice said behind me. It sounded familiar, but when I turned around, I faced a teenage boy I'd never seen before in my life. And believe me, if I had seen him before, I would have remembered. He was a little too skinny, but it was easy to forget that while peering into his glowing green eyes, then casting my gaze over his perfect features, his flawless skin, his muscular frame. . . . I wouldn't have thought anyone could make a boring hospital gown look attractive, but this guy did.

"Who are you?" Edwy asked.

"I save your life and you forget me two hours later?" the boy asked.

And suddenly I knew why his voice sounded familiar.

"Alcibiades?" I said.

CHAPTER FORTY-FOUR

"Kiandra?" the boy said, sounding just as hesitant as I did. He looked back and forth between Edwy, Rosi, and me, as if he couldn't tell us apart. "I—I never thought you'd look like that with tentacles. . . ."

"Tentacles?" I repeated stupidly.

"You see us looking like Zacadians, and we see you looking human?" Edwy cracked up. "This is really funny!"

"Um . . . ," I began. Looking directly at Alcibiades was a little like looking directly at the sun.

It's not real, it's not real, it's not real. . . .

"I always thought you were an old man!" I protested. "I mean, not that I knew anything about judging Zacadian ages, and I guess I never asked, but . . . I thought you'd been in that prison for eons! You acted like you knew everything!"

"None of our old people survived," Alcibiades said grimly. "They had to pass on their knowledge before they expired."

Now a rueful smile teased at his mouth. "I hadn't actually ever flown a spaceship before. I just had my people's stories guiding me."

"I'm kind of glad I didn't know that six days ago," Rosi murmured.

"What other choice did we have, except to trust Alcibiades?" Edwy asked.

"None," Rosi said briskly. "But now we have lots of choices. And we need to make the best one. So—"

"Please wake up Enu, so we can all go talk to the intergalactic court," Cana finished for her.

The healer pursed her lips and looked torn. Cana had a way of gazing up beseechingly that almost always worked on me, even in my darkest moments trapped in the Zacadi prison. Wouldn't Cana's secret weapon work even better on someone whose whole life purpose was empathy?

"All right," the healer decided. "I'll let you go talk to the officials over in that area, to get on their agenda. But Enu will need to stay in a wheelchair, and it's straight back to bed if I think there's any threat to his health."

It took time to summon an orderly to move Enu to a wheelchair. I didn't *think* the healer was delaying on purpose, but she was agonizingly slow consulting a wrist computer about the best way to rouse Enu again. I studied Alcibiades out of the corner of my eye while we all waited.

"Were your eyes green before and I just never noticed?" I asked him.

"Green?" He sounded surprised. "Of all the questions . . . Hmm. I don't know. You may have noticed that there weren't any mirrors in my prison cell. Why? Does it matter?"

"It doesn't," Rosi said firmly.

"But some people on Earth think it does," Edwy added.

"Now, now." The healer looked up from her wrist computer. "Arguments like that could get our patient too agitated again. You *all* are still under medical observation, and need to avoid challenging situations. *Her* blood pressure just shot up in a worrisome fashion. I can tell."

She was pointing at me.

"We're not arguing," I told the healer. "And I'm fine. Have you never dealt with people who have been through really bad experiences before?"

"I've *studied* every medical possibility," the healer said defensively. "I'm a fully trained healer. You needn't worry that my care will be inadequate."

"That wasn't what I was implying at all," I said. I was on good behavior—I didn't roll my eyes. How had Edwy and Rosi survived twelve years in Fredtown, being around people like this?

I turned back to Alcibiades.

"I'm not one of the people who care about green eyes," I said hastily. "I was just wondering."

"How does it work?" Rosi asked the healer. "The appearance switching, I mean. If somebody was here who really hated people with green eyes, would they see Alcibiades's eyes as brown instead?"

"Or blue or gray or purple?" It figured Edwy would want to complicate things.

The healer furrowed her brow.

"I—I've never thought to wonder such a thing," she admitted.

Alcibiades clutched his head in his hands.

"You all *look* like you have tentacles, and you're speaking Zacadian, but nothing you're saying makes any sense!" he complained.

Just then a robot orderly slipped into the room. He gently lifted Enu from the bed and settled him into a wheelchair. The healer tucked a blanket around him and began rubbing a thick paste onto his forehead.

"By the time his skin absorbs this, he'll be clearheaded and alert again," she said. "But it should also give him a lingering sense of peace and calm."

Enu's eyelids fluttered.

"Where . . . am I?" he said groggily. "What's going on? I dreamed . . ."

His eyes came all the way open. He stared confusedly at the healer bent over him. Then suddenly he shoved the wheelchair back and bolted to his feet. He waved his arms wildly, the way someone might panic and shove away imaginary spiders or snakes.

"The Enforcers are chasing us! We're all going to die if we don't fight back!"

I rushed to his side.

"Enu, stop it!" I cried. "We're not on Zacadi anymore. You've been unconscious for days! We'll explain everything, but—"

"Young man!" the healer interrupted. "Peace and calm! That was a double dose! You should not even be capable of swinging your arms like that right now!"

The healer reached for his bandaged shoulder, which, I saw, was starting to bleed again. But before she could touch him, Enu's flailing fist smashed against the healer's face and knocked her to the floor.

She didn't get back up.

CHAPTER
FORTY-FIVE

Enu dropped his arms and stared down at the healer like he couldn't understand what had happened.

"I—I thought she was an Enforcer," he said. "My eyes weren't working right. I . . ."

I was too frozen to do anything, but Rosi shoved past us both.

"Is the healer all right?" she shrieked. "We should call somebody! We should—"

Edwy ran over and clapped his hand over her mouth.

At the same time, the robot orderly rolled forward, a beam of light shooting from its head along the healer's body.

"Subject is merely unconscious," the robot reported in an emotionless voice. "No permanent damage done. Healing will occur while subject sleeps. Sending accident report and related request for—"

Before I could quite follow his action, Alcibiades dived across the room, grabbed the robot orderly, and slashed his hand down the robot's back and front. Maybe its sides and head as well.

"—forrrrr zzzzzzz. Self-shut-down procedure begun."

The robot orderly sagged to the floor as well, right beside the healer.

"You shut it off?" I accused Alcibiades. No way could he have acted that quickly using only two hands. He must have really used multiple tentacles, but my eyes hadn't let me see it that way. "Did you manage to stop it *before* the accident report went through or *after*?"

"Hard to tell," Alcibiades said through gritted teeth.

He edged away from Enu, who was still confusedly blinking and peering around, even if he'd stopped swinging his fists. Then Enu's gaze locked on Alcibiades.

"Do we even know you?" Enu asked.

I stepped between the two of them, just in case Enu got any bright ideas about punching Alcibiades, too.

"He's a friend," I told Enu sternly. "I'll explain later."

Rosi and Cana slid a pillow under the healer's head. To my surprise, Edwy pulled a blanket off the bed to cover her as well.

Alcibiades darted back to the door and peeked out.

"We have to go before anyone comes," he said, glancing back over his shoulder at the rest of us. "Otherwise, they'll want us to explain *this*"—he pointed at the healer—"and there isn't time. Not if we have any hope of saving any of my people."

I remembered the Zacadians falling before the Enforcers' guns as we ran for the spaceship. How long had that gone on? How many Zacadians were even left?

How about the humans who'd been sent to Zacadi? Or the humans who'd been left on Earth under the Enforcers' cruel siege?

Udans, Bobo, Zeba, Mom, Dad . . .

"Here's what we should do," I began. "Edwy, Rosi, and Cana, why don't the three of you stay here and explain, while Enu, Alcibiades, and I go talk with the intergalactic court? Or—"

"We're going with you," Rosi said firmly as she rose to her feet. "The healer will be okay. And the intergalactic court needs to hear what we have to say too."

I stood back, my hands up like I was surrendering.

"All right," I said. "I wouldn't try to stop you."

"The hallway's clear," Alcibiades reported, waving a hand over his shoulder. "Come on."

I took Enu's arm.

"Don't hit anyone else," I told him. Then I amended: "I mean, not unless you have to. Do you need a wheelchair, or are you okay to walk?"

"Walk," Enu mumbled. "Need to walk off . . . daze . . ."

Enu kept blinking and stumbling, veering side to side. I had to hold on tight.

"Feel . . . so weird," Enu groaned. "Can't get my eyes to work right. . . . Are we . . . safe here?"

I considered that.

"I think *we* are. For now. It's the rest of humanity we're worried about. And the Zacadians."

"The slimy tentacle creatures?" Enu mumbled. He looked around, confusion on his face. "Didn't we escape them? In my nightmares I kept running and running and running. . . ."

It was hard to tell what he remembered of the Zacadians curing him, and Alcibiades carrying us to the spaceship. Maybe he thought all of it was just a nightmare. But there wasn't time to explain everything right now. And he was so groggy, I wasn't sure he'd understand anyway.

"Just stick with me," I said. "We'll be fine." Enu and I never got mushy, but I couldn't help it now. I gave his arm a squeeze. "I'm just glad you're alive."

The two of us stepped out into the hall, right behind Alcibiades, Edwy, Rosi, and Cana. I almost wanted to giggle, the way all of us shifted into innocent-looking saunters once we were out in the open.

Well, that was the way Cana and Rosi walked all the time, but it was fake for the rest of us.

Just as fake as Enforcers or Freds who look like humans, or a hospital room on this planet that looks like my room at home . . .

I was working toward something with that thought, but I was still a little groggy myself. It was a struggle just to concentrate on walking and helping Enu along.

The hallway was bland and boring and long. Alcibiades dropped back to walk alongside Enu and me.

"I thought there'd be signs somewhere, telling how to get to the intergalactic court chambers," he whispered. "My grandparents, my aunts and uncles—they said that's how government buildings were, back when Zacadi had government buildings. They said if I ever got to plead our case, that's what I should look for. . . ."

"Alcibiades, were you *born* in that prison cell?" I asked. "Had you lived your whole life there?"

"Pretty much," he said grimly.

That explained why his eyes were darting about so desperately now, why he seemed to have to try so hard to hide his complete befuddlement.

"I know what to do," I said, trying to sound confident.

The next time we reached a doorway leading into another hospital room, I poked my head inside. My gamble paid off: A healer stood on duty in a little alcove. She seemed to be going through medical records for the very ancient man lying in the hospital bed in the room beyond.

"Excuse me," I said. "I am *so* sorry to bother you. My friends and I have been summoned to speak in the intergalactic court chambers, but we got *completely* turned around. I don't know *how* we ended up here in the hospital wing." Oops—not a convincing lie if she noticed that Enu was behind me wearing a hospital gown. But who knew how she actually saw any of us. If my eyes made my brain think she was human, did she see me and think we were covered with Fred fur? Maybe she didn't even see us as wearing clothes.

Stop thinking about that, or about how differently Freds see things. . . .

I decided to act as though I thought I was telling the truth, and maybe that would convince her. I pasted on a fake smile.

"Could you just give us directions to the court chambers, and we'll be out of your way?" Edwy added, right at my elbow. He finished with a smile that was just as sickly sweet and mock-sincere as mine.

For a kid raised in Fredtown, he was an amazing liar.

"Well, of course," the healer said, beaming kindly back at us. "You poor things. I know it takes months to get an appointment to speak to the court, and they only summon the most important speakers. . . . How stressful it must be to have gotten turned around today of all days. Here. I'll print you a map."

She typed a few commands into the computer before her.

I concentrated on not letting my face show how distressed I was by her words: *It takes months to get an appointment.* The healer Enu had punched had probably planned to explain that to us too. No wonder she'd finally agreed to let us go— she thought we were only going to sign up for the *chance* to go before the court someday far in the future.

But we had to find a way to speak to the court today. We'd already wasted enough time.

A paper came chugging out of the side of this healer's computer, and she handed it to me.

"The X is where we are now, and if you head on down the hall, you'll turn at the collection of red balloons. . . ." The healer pointed out landmarks on the map. "You see how everything is linked in the court complex—it's really simple to get around."

"Thank you, ma'am," Rosi said, adding her own glowing smile.

The healer went back to her medical records, and all six of us kids continued down the hall.

Alcibiades waited until we were several steps away from the healer before he whispered, "It's like she didn't suspect a thing! Are Freds stupid? Is that the problem?"

"Not stupid—innocent," Rosi whispered back. "It would never occur to her to lie, so she couldn't even consider that we might be lying."

"The Freds back in Fredtown always knew when I was lying," Edwy countered ruefully.

"That's because your Fred-parents and teachers had been around *you* enough to understand that lies were possible," Rosi told him. But there was no barb to her words—she almost sounded nostalgic.

"See? I trained them!" Edwy said. "They should thank me!"

"But what are the Freds on the court like?" Alcibiades asked. "I've only ever dealt with Enforcers and my fellow Zacadians—and now you humans. How are we supposed to convince species we don't know anything about that the Enforcers must be stopped?"

"Rosi, Cana, and I know all about the Freds," Edwy bragged.

"Freds," Enu said darkly, as if he was just starting to put his thoughts back together. "Hate Freds."

"They really do mean well," Rosi said, as if that could convince us to forgive them.

We kept walking, all of us lost in our own thoughts. We turned at the red balloons, and faced another long hallway. But at least the doors we passed now looked less like hospital rooms and more like business offices.

"Can we trust anything we see around us?" I asked. "If Alcibiades looks like a green-eyed human to us, and we look like nine-tentacled Zacadians to him, then—"

"I don't see all of you as having nine tentacles," Alcibiades interrupted. "Females always have more—usually eleven or twelve by the time they're grown." He pointed first to Cana, then to Rosi, then to me. "You have five, you have ten, and you have, um, your full twelve."

Just the way he said "twelve" made me blush. I guess while I was seeing him as a really, really hot human, maybe he was seeing me as a really, really hot Zacadian.

Then Cana piped up, "Is it magic? The way all of us see other people differently?" She studied Alcibiades. "I think you have purple eyes, not green." She tilted her head and said solemnly, "I like purple."

So whatever causes this takes our preferences into account? I thought. *And, being raised in Fredtown, Cana never learned the prejudice about green eyes being best?*

"It's not magic," Edwy said. "It's not elaborate disguises, either, like what the Freds used back in Fredtown."

"Or what the Enforcers used on Earth and Zacadi," I muttered. "If you looked hard enough, you could tell those were fake. But this . . ."

I sneaked another glance at Alcibiades. He looked completely human. Completely, amazingly human.

"Yeah," Edwy agreed. "I asked my healer how the system works here. He said the air in the intergalactic court complex has genetically altered microbes in it, and those microbes circle around us and filter the light that gets into our eyes, which changes what we see."

That must be the "protocols" the Enforcers who met our spaceship were talking about, I thought. *They meant that that microbe air flowed into our spaceship, too, because we were at an intergalactic-court docking station.*

I had to hold back a shiver thinking about those Enforcers. But if they'd turned us over to the Freds who healed us, were they as bad as the Enforcers we'd encountered on Earth and Zacadi?

Or is there still more about the intergalactic court that I don't understand?

Beside me, Rosi clapped a hand over her mouth in horror.

"Are you saying those microbes read our minds?" she asked.

"No, just our reactions," Edwy said. "At least, that's what the healer told me."

Could we believe that?

"So if I get close enough to Alcibiades and his specialized microbes—sorry, Alcibiades—will I see everything the way he does?" I asked. As I spoke, I moved closer to him, practically pressing my head against his. To my great disappointment, I did not suddenly see my brothers and the two girls with multiple tentacles. Everyone and everything looked the same as before.

"I tried that with my healer, too, and it didn't work," Edwy said. "These are really, really advanced microbes. It takes years of training to know how to shut them off, even for a minute."

"Can we walk faster, and worry about all of this later?" Alcibiades asked.

I squinted—just in an instant he'd moved far ahead of the rest of us. I wanted so badly to be able to see the tentacles that were really propelling him forward. The harder I watched, the more his human-looking legs blurred together. But I couldn't make myself see them as tentacles.

"Do you think they have guards standing outside the courtroom?" Cana asked, stretching her legs to try to keep up. "Do you think those guards are Enforcers? Why would they let us in to say bad things about other Enforcers?"

How could a little kid like her be asking about magic one moment, and figuring out the holes in our plan the next?

"Lie," Enu said, still weaving unsteadily. "We have to lie."

Cana *didn't* immediately counter, *But lying is wrong! We're not supposed to lie! Here are fifty principles of Fredtown about why people shouldn't lie!* And I felt an odd pang, as though I was sad that Cana had grown up, that Cana had been corrupted. I'd seen her change just in the time I'd known her.

"I wish we still had some of those exploding pearls," Edwy said.

259

"I bet I could find some," Alcibiades said.

He reached up to one of the glowing lights that lined the hallway and twisted the base of the orb. The light went out, and he pulled out what looked like a large grain of sand.

"Back home we call this a pearl tenth," he said. "It's a tenth of a normal-size Zacadi pearl."

Rosi all but began clapping.

"How did you know that would be there?" she asked.

"Every bit of territory under the jurisdiction of the intergalactic court runs on Zacadi pearls," Alcibiades said.

"*We* didn't have that on Earth," I said.

"And either we didn't have them in Fredtown, or they were always hidden," Edwy said. "Zacadi pearls were something else the Freds didn't tell us about."

Alcibiades shrugged.

"Didn't you say humans were just probationary members of the court before the Enforcers came?" he asked. "That's why you didn't have them. Believe me, the intergalactic court wouldn't have given them to us Zacadians, either, if the pearls hadn't come from our planet. But having access— that's one of the biggest benefits of being full members of the court. Didn't you know that?"

He sounded proud and bitter and sorrowful, all at once.

Because if Zacadi pearls are that important to the intergalactic court, I thought, *doesn't that mean that all their territories are dependent on the Enforcers using slave labor to mine them?*

What if the Freds already knew what was happening on Zacadi—and Earth—and just didn't care? What hope did we have then?

The rest of the group ran to the next light, to help Alcibiades collect another tenth of a pearl. And my feet made me follow along.

My feet, at least, had hope.

CHAPTER
FORTY-SIX

Edwy, it turned out, was good at spying.

As we got close to the area of our map labeled INTERGALACTIC COURT CHAMBERS, he began holding us back at every doorway and intersecting hallway, and then tiptoeing forward only after one of us could peek out and make sure the coast was clear. Finally we reached a corner that led to a pair of imposing stairways. By bending low and looking up, we could just barely see that the stairways joined again two flights up, in front of an arched doorway guarded by men in dark uniforms.

This was the entry to the intergalactic court.

Edwy held the rest of us back.

"I'll tiptoe over to hide under that banister and count the guards," he whispered.

"No, I should do it," Cana said. "I'm the smallest, and if they catch me, I'll just say I'm lost. They'll believe me."

She smiled up at us, and it was horrible, but we let her go.

She put her thumb in her mouth before she stepped around the corner, and instantly looked even younger than five.

She seemed to be making no attempt whatsoever to crouch down or hide.

"Hey! Hey! Who are you? This is a prohibited zone! You don't have authorization to be here!" a gruff voice yelled almost instantly from above.

I froze, but Cana just turned her head slowly and gazed innocently up the stairs. She took a few casual steps up, as if she was only trying to see who had called out to her.

"My mommy is in the in-ter-guh-lac-tic court," she said, pronouncing each syllable separately, as if she were proud she could say such a big word. "I was in her office, and I got bored waiting."

"Well, you need to go back! Now!"

This was another voice, even sterner and gruffer.

"Okay," Cana said. Even from the side, I could see how innocently she blinked her eyes. "I didn't mean to break any rules."

But when she stepped back down, she kept walking forward, instead of turning around. She scuffed the toes of her shoes against the marble floor; she danced and skipped. She looked like a carefree, careless kid.

I heard footsteps on the staircase and caught my breath.

Alcibiades, Edwy, Enu, Rosi, and I all clung together, poised to run if we had to—either to dart out and rescue Cana, or to flee to save ourselves.

"Kid!" The voice rang out way too close. "To go back to your mommy's office, you have to *turn around*! Go back the way you came! *Not* the long way around. Now get out of here! Scram!"

I couldn't see the yelling guard. But I imagined him poised halfway down the stairs, his gun pointed at Cana.

Cana turned and stared up the stairs again. Her eyes stayed wide and innocent.

"Ooooh," she breathed. "I didn't know what you meant before."

"That way!" The guard must have pointed, but Cana was slow about spinning on her heel and trudging back toward us. She clasped her hands together behind her back like a little kid who was in no hurry to get anywhere.

Only when she reached the wall where the rest of us were hiding did her expression change from innocent and aimless to tense and excited.

"The guard didn't suspect *anything*!" she announced.

"Shh," I warned her. I pressed my ear against the wall, listening.

For a moment nothing happened. Then there were footsteps. Footsteps headed *up* the stairs, not farther down.

"And it's pretty clear that that guard was an Enforcer or some similar species," Rosi muttered. "Any Fred or Fred-like creature would have helped a lost little kid get back where she belonged."

"Well, it's good for us that the guard didn't care," Edwy said.

"You mean *guards*," Cana corrected. "There were six of them in front of the doors at the top of the stairs."

"Guards," Enu grunted. "Hate guards. Want to—"

"No punching unless you have to, remember?" I grabbed his arm just in case he planned to dart out and attack the guard immediately.

Enu clutched his head.

"So . . . confused. You'll tell me when it's time to punch, right?" he asked, and for a moment it was like we were little kids again, totally relying on each other.

"Don't worry. I will," I said.

"On to the next part of the plan, then," Alcibiades said grimly.

Cana began jumping up and down, just as merrily as when she was pretending for the guards.

"Oh, but I *already* did the next step." Cana whispered, but it still sounded like she was crowing with joy. "When I put my hands behind my back, I dropped one Zacadi pearl tenth after another. So now we're ready for the fun part."

I'm not sure whose jaw dropped the farthest in astonishment.

"Wow, Cana," Edwy said. "If you ever want to be a criminal mastermind like my father—like Enu's, Kiandra's, and my father—then—"

"She does *not* want to be a criminal mastermind," Rosi snapped. "She only wants to be sneaky for a good cause. Right, Cana?"

"Oh, right," Cana agreed.

"Well, let's hope it works," Alcibiades said, in a way that made me see him as incredibly ancient again, even though all his features were so young and handsome. He still had old, sad eyes.

"Does everybody remember their assigned role?" I asked.

The others nodded.

Rosi and Alcibiades crouched side by side by the corner. We'd decided they would be best at this part. They divided up what was left of the Zacadi pearl tenths we'd gathered.

"One, two, three . . . go!" Rosi whispered, even as both she and Alcibiades arced their arms back.

And then both of them launched their arms forward and threw one pearl tenth after another.

At first nothing happened, but then we heard the first explosion at the bottom of the far staircase. A second, third, and fourth sounded before I lost count. Then . . . silence.

"Go, go, go, go . . . ," Edwy whispered.

Alcibiades and Rosi sprang up. All six of us began running for the stairway that hadn't been destroyed.

"Guards! Guards!" I shouted up the stairs. "We saw who did that! You have to let us into the courtroom to tell!"

CHAPTER FORTY-SEVEN

Would it work?

While I raced up the first flight of stairs, I caught only quick glimpses around. I saw a crazy, quick snippet of the stairs beneath my feet and on up to the door: *Okay, good, this side isn't damaged. There's a clear path up.* I saw my friends and brothers around me: *Yes, we're all together. Everyone's keeping up. Even Enu.* And I saw the guards above us: *Four are running toward the exploded staircase, so we won't have to worry about them. It's only the two still standing by the door that we have to convince, only those two we have to fool. . . .*

They'd never suspect that *we* were the guilty parties, would they? Surely they'd never imagine that anyone would commit a crime and then be crazy enough to run straight to the authorities, instead of running away.

Surely they didn't understand how devious humans could be, did they?

It felt like I was staking my life on that. On their not understanding.

My feet kept propelling me up and up and up the stairs, closer and closer and closer to the guards.

We reached the first landing and sprinted for the next flight of stairs. I let the others take up my cries: "We can tell the court everything!" "We know exactly what happened!" "We saw where the bad guys went after the explosion!"

When we got to the second landing, the remaining two guards stood directly in front of us—and in front of the courtroom door. They hadn't budged. I pretended to be surprised.

"Didn't you hear?" I cried. "We have to report to the court! Let us in! No—escort us in, so we're sure it's safe in *there*."

It was a calculated risk. For a moment the guards only glared at me. Their eyes looked human—glittering and dark, but human all the same. Of course I knew their appearance was just an illusion, just a trick, and I felt certain that they were really Enforcers. I could feel the same chill I'd felt the first time I'd met an Enforcer; I felt the same desire to turn around and flee.

But I glared back, and the guards actually pushed open the door for us.

"You have to listen to us!" I screamed, stalking through the doorway. "We've got information the intergalactic court has to hear!"

At least a hundred shocked pairs of eyes stared back at us. Like the guards—like everyone we'd met since landing—the court members who were sitting in a semicircle before us all appeared entirely human. They had green or brown or blue or gray eyes; they had two arms, two legs, and a single head; they wore the same kind of business suits I wouldn't have glanced at twice back in Refuge City, back home. They all looked so familiar.

And maybe that did help. I gathered the courage to keep moving. All six of us kids marched down the center aisle of the room. We reached a low wooden railing. Nobody stopped Alcibiades from yanking open the latched part of the railing; nobody stopped the six of us from racing on up to the podium in the center of the stage beyond. The podium was framed by ten glowing orbs—five on each side. Back in Refuge City, back on Earth, I had tried to avoid any information I could about the intergalactic court. But even I knew those ten globes were the symbols of the court, representing the ten original civilizations that had joined together for peace and harmony throughout the universe.

Yeah, right, I thought.

I had to look away from the globes. To steady myself, I fixed my gaze on the huge window behind the stage, showing the lush jungle scenery outside. After our time out in the desert on Earth and in the ruined wasteland of Zacadi, the greenery outdoors looked like paradise.

But I had to turn away from the window, too, and face the staring eyes.

Alcibiades was already stepping up to the podium.

"You have information about the explosions?" someone called out to him. It might have been one of the guards. "Do we need to evacuate?"

"I have information . . . ," Alcibiades began, "*related* to those explosions. You're safe here and now. But we bring you distressing news from the outer planets. From Zacadi and Earth."

A roar of discontented grumbling rose from the crowd. I tried to see who looked angry and who looked concerned— would that be a way to discover which of the people before us were Enforcers and which were Freds? But my vision blurred, the faces before me too fake to decipher.

If I couldn't even see what species sat before me, how could I expect to figure out their emotions? Or what would work to convince them?

"We have official ambassadors representing Earth and Zacadi," someone shouted. "You are only children. We have rules—we hear reports only from the official ambassadors or their designees."

Okay, that was probably an Enforcer saying that, trying to get us off the stage, I thought.

"But your official ambassadors from our planets are Enforcers," Alcibiades protested. "And our complaints are against Enforcers. We are Zacadians and humans who have been sorely treated by Enforcers, in violation of everything the intergalactic court stands for."

That set off a buzz. Alcibiades certainly had a way with words—or, at least, in the way his words were translated for my ears. What were the Freds and the Enforcers hearing?

I had no control over the way anything was translated, but I listened hard, trying to pull out individual reactions from the hubbub.

"This is ridiculous!" a man ranted. "Have we no standards now? We'll let any random creature interrupt us and hold our proceedings hostage?"

"Don't we have an age limit for our speakers?" a woman shrieked. "So we're not subjected to the babbling of infants?"

They're both Enforcers, I thought, with a sinking heart. *Are Enforcers the only ones who speak on the court?*

But then I heard an undertone of softer mumblings: ". . . those poor children look so sad." "Can you imagine the courage it would take for mere tykes to stand up there and . . ." "That boy certainly *seems* sincere. . . ."

I leaned in beside Alcibiades and tried my own appeal.

"The intergalactic court claims to speak for truth and justice throughout the universe, and we bring you truth the official ambassadors would not reveal," I said. I reached into the back pocket of my shorts and pulled out my phone. "And we bring you proof."

CHAPTER
FORTY-EIGHT

The buzz of outraged voices grew louder. How much time did I have? Alcibiades pressed the last Zacadi pearl tenth we'd commandeered into my hand. I just needed to figure out how to trick the phone into using that as an energy source, to give the phone enough juice to come back to life. Then I needed to figure out how to cue up the video I'd taken way back in Refuge City right before the Enforcers captured us, and figure out how to project that video onto the wall of the courtroom. . . .

One step at a time, I told myself.

Rosi stretched up to the podium while Alcibiades and I struggled over the phone. Edwy lifted Cana in his arms, holding her up beside Rosi, facing the microphone. Distantly I heard a few oohs and aahs and mumbled comments: "Oh, isn't the little one cute? Small ones of any species are adorable!"

It really made me want to tell them the "adorable" little one's role in blowing up their staircase. But I had to focus on the phone.

"Edwy, Cana, and I were among the children raised in a Fredtown and returned to Earth," Rosi began in a trembling voice. Behind the podium I saw Edwy sneak his hand into hers, and Rosi went on. "In the beginning, knowing nothing of Earth, it was hard for us to understand why our parents there were meaner than our Fred-parents. We knew nothing of our own history. I tried to help Edwy, and people thought I was trying to start a riot, trying to start another war."

Gasps greeted her last word, as if it was normally too horrifying even to mention such violence in the court chambers.

Oh, just wait, I thought, fumbling with the casing of my phone.

"The Enforcers put me in prison in a place called Cursed Town, but kind and loyal humans—including my own parents—helped me escape," Rosi continued.

More gasps. A voice rang out, "*She's* the famous Cursed Town escapee? Then we're listening to criminals! Convicts! How can we believe a word they say?"

Um, Rosi, did you have to mention that?

I was still trying to wedge the tiny piece of Zacadi pearl into the phone. What if the intergalactic court kicked us out—and back to the Enforcer guards—before I could show the video?

Edwy stepped forward, as though he enjoyed talking to angry people.

"I *know!*" he said. "Rosi *can* be really annoying, because she tries so hard to do what's right. But is that any reason to put someone in jail for the rest of her life? Without a trial? I didn't pay attention to much of anything the Freds told me at school, but I thought people were always supposed to have the right to tell their side of a story, any time they were accused of anything. Those poor Freds in my Fredtown had to listen to me constantly, telling all my reasons for dyeing our pet dog blue, or writing invisible-ink messages that made fun of our teachers, or, well, pulling Rosi's hair. . . ."

Part of the crowd laughed, and part of the crowd gasped.

Oh, Edwy, you're a genius, I thought. *People are going to keep listening, just to see what you'll say next!* Now I had the Zacadi pearl solidly in place. A light flickered on the phone's screen, then vanished. I pressed the back of the phone harder. *Come on, come on, come on. . . .*

"In Fredtown, I thought everything Edwy did was bad," Rosi admitted, her gaze gliding over everyone before us. "But sometimes he was just curious, and the Freds wouldn't give us answers. Back on Earth he was really, really brave, and he saved my life. And Cana's. He's a mix of good and bad. Just like all humans. Wouldn't you rather have us doing good things in the galaxy, instead of giving us more and more reasons to rebel?"

I aimed the phone at the wall even as I typed commands into the screen. *See, Enu*, I wanted to say, *this is why I always check out every possible function every time I get a new device. Just in case I need to do something unusual in a hurry.*

But Enu already had his fists half raised, as if he couldn't understand how to do anything but fight.

"Enu," I whispered. "No punching, remember? This is what we wanted to do all along. Show the intergalactic court this video."

I hit the last keystroke, and an image appeared on the wall: The dark street back in Refuge City, and the shadowy Enforcers who'd invaded its peace.

I adjusted the lighting of the video so everything showed up clearly, and that was enough to bring tears to my eyes. If I looked past the Enforcers, I could see how beautiful, how hopeful, how human my old home was. Even in my pathetically inadequate school, we'd studied our city's history. I'd always known that Refuge City had come into existence because of war, and because of humans wanting to move past their wars and start something new and better. But I'd never understood how defiant everything was: the curlicues on the iron railings on every balcony, the ridiculously bright clothing people wore, the skyscrapers themselves. All of those things said that humans wanted to be more than warriors, more than war-haunted victims.

Then there was the way the woman caught in my video sheltered her little boy beside her, even as Enforcers' fists pounded against her body.

Tears began to stream down my face, and I didn't wipe them away.

I'd had only a moment to film the beating before the phone had been invisibly jerked from my hand and suspended above my head. Once that happened, I had stopped watching the beating and focused on reaching for the phone. But to my surprise, the phone had kept recording. On the balcony—and now, projected on the wall of the intergalactic court—the woman coiled her body to the side, so the Enforcers' blows hit her back and not her stomach. And as she turned, I saw why.

"She's pregnant!" I screamed at the intergalactic court. "The Enforcers that *you* sent to Earth were beating a pregnant woman! It's right there in front of you!"

The video went blurry and then dark. I remembered how the phone had fallen and I'd caught it and then stuffed it into my pocket.

"Do you need to see that again?" I shouted. "Do you need to see more of what the Enforcers have done in your name? You have to stop them!"

I stared out into the crowd, trying again to pick out which of the human-looking creatures before me were actually Freds and which were Enforcers. I tried to read the faces: Who was most distressed? Who would stride forward and come to my aid?

Who would be the hero?

But the faces before me looked merely . . . uncertain. Confused.

A man stood at the front and waved a hand to the side the same way someone might shoo away a fly.

"Didn't you hear these children say they are *humans*?" he asked. "Remember, humans are tricksters. You've heard how they can fake any sort of scene for their movies and video games. They're *entertained* by violence. This is just more of their fakery. I assure you, nothing like this is *actually* happening on Earth. Or anywhere under our control."

Murmurs flowed through the crowd. But they weren't murmurs of disbelief or complaint. They were mutterings of "Oh, that's right" and "What a relief" and "Why are these children wasting our time?"

Even when I had proof, the intergalactic court didn't believe me.

CHAPTER
FORTY-NINE

"**What can we do** now?" Edwy moaned beside me.

Alcibiades stepped up to the podium.

"But you haven't heard my story," he said. "I am not human. I am Zacadian, and it is my planet's resources that fuel your expansion throughout the universe. It is my people's slave labor and nearing extinction that should weigh on your consciences. . . ."

Even when Alcibiades spoke the words "slave labor" and "extinction," the faces before me kept their bland expressions. The court looked, at worst, vaguely annoyed. Maybe there were no translations for those terms in the Fred language, in the Enforcer language. Maybe when the Freds saw Alcibiades as a fuzzy blue creature, like a cuddly stuffed animal, they just couldn't understand the horror his species had endured. Maybe they couldn't see how emaciated he was, how he'd almost starved. Or how *all* of us had almost starved.

How long did we have before the intergalactic court just shooed all of us away?

How could we get through to the intergalactic court when they couldn't even see us clearly—or see one another clearly? How could the Freds on the court blame the Enforcers on the court when the Enforcers looked like kindly, fuzzy blue and green creatures, too?

My eyes fell on the row of ten glowing orbs between us and the members of the court, and suddenly I knew what I had to do. I reached for the orb nearest me, but my arms felt rubbery. Even before my weeks of slave labor and starvation on Zacadi, I'd never been an athlete; I'd never had Enu's muscles.

I knew what to do, but I needed Enu's help.

"Enu, do you trust me?" I whispered to my brother, while Alcibiades continued his useless appeal to the court.

"Trust you?" Enu mumbled back. "Is it time to punch someone?"

He raised his fists, and I had to shove his hands back down.

"Not punch," I whispered back. "Throw. Do you think you're strong enough to lift this orb?"

Keeping my hands low, so no one out in the court area could see, I pointed and pantomimed to Enu what I wanted him to do.

Enu's eyes widened. And he never even asked, *Are you sure?* or *Have you thought this one through?* or *Are you crazy?*

He just grabbed the orb from its stand, gripped it like a toddler carrying a bowling ball, and whirled around to hurl it at the window behind us.

CHAPTER FIFTY

The glass shuddered, and for a split second I feared Enu hadn't thrown the ball hard enough. I yanked at the next orb, ready to throw it, and saw that Edwy, Rosi, and Alcibiades followed suit. They trusted me too. Or they'd also figured out what I was trying to do. A volley of orbs sailed toward the window—tossed by Alcibiades's multiple tentacles? Or just us puny humans all working together? I couldn't tell which globe made the first crack in the glass, or which was the first to crash through.

But a hole appeared in the glass, and then the glass shattered completely. I felt a whoosh of air leave the room, and sirens began wailing around us.

"Can we breathe if . . . ?" Edwy asked beside me, but I didn't listen. I was too busy gaping at the scene revealed on the other side of the window: The lush, junglelike greenery had vanished, replaced by a landscape just as dead and lifeless as the desert on Earth back home, or the destroyed Zacadi land we'd been forced to mine.

"Even that was a lie!" I screamed. I pointed out the glass-less window and yelled over my shoulder toward the court, "Now you have to see things as they really are!"

The members of the court were screaming so loudly themselves, I'm sure no one heard me. I turned back toward them, and they had all been transformed: Human shapes had scrunched down into fuzzy blue and green and purple creatures, or stretched out into hard-shelled, overgrown bee-tles, or morphed into species that either lacked arms and legs or had too many appendages to count. . . . The variety was dazzling. Even Alcibiades was transformed back to his nor-mal multitentacled glory. I grinned at him, then drew in a breath to scream to the members of the court before us, "And is that what all of you look like? Really?"

But what I inhaled wasn't air. Maybe it was more like water. Maybe it wasn't anything.

Edwy's question finally registered: *Can we breathe if . . . ?*

No need to finish the rest of the sentence.

No. The answer was no.

I tried to hold my breath, tried not to let out any oxygen I'd managed to trap in my lungs before breaking the window. But it was too late. My vision began to slip into darkness.

And then something hit me on the head.

CHAPTER
FIFTY-ONE

Alcibiades saved me. He saved all of us humans.

He was still alert enough to realize that emergency breathing packets were falling from the ceiling, like hundreds of emergency oxygen masks on airplanes. Watching the members of the court snatch up the packets and press them against their arms—or legs or tentacles or, well, whatever—he snatched up a handful and pressed one against his own face, one on my shoulder, one on Cana's wrist, one on Enu's neck, and the last two on Rosi's cheek and Edwy's forehead.

They all worked.

"Okay, I hope you all understand that we were *not* trying to kill anyone, because of course that would have killed us as well, and nobody would do *that*," Rosi said, scrambling toward the podium to try to explain.

"If you have to blame somebody, blame me," I said, stepping past her.

I dared to look out at the crowd, and it seemed as though

the Enforcers and the other stern-looking creatures were gathering to storm toward us. Then the fuzzy creatures—the Freds, and others who looked similar—formed a line along the railings. What good would that do? The Enforcers and their friends ran toward the Freds, and I expected them to break through easily. I braced to fight. Even if it was an unwinnable battle, I planned to go down swinging.

But the Enforcers bounced back as soon as they reached the Freds.

Could it be that the Freds were actually more powerful than the Enforcers?

"Why did you ever let the Enforcers have *any* power?" I started to scream at them.

But as I watched, something happened to the creatures before me. The air seemed clearer than ever. Maybe it was because the original air in the chamber had vanished completely, along with all the genetically altered microbes that had changed my vision. Now some of the fuzzy creatures seemed to lose parts of their fur, with beetlelike scales showing through instead. And some of the beetlelike creatures— the ones I'd taken for more Enforcers—seemed to grow fur on their arms, their stomachs, their foreheads. In seconds, almost all the creatures before us—both the ones protecting us and the ones who'd seemed intent on attacking us—displayed a mix of traits, scaly and fuzzy all at once.

And now all the creatures began screaming the way I'd expected them to when I showed the video: "No!" "It's not possible!" "This can't be!"

And then there was an overwhelming roar of lots of creatures screaming variations of the same words: "I can't be seen like this!"

In a panic they all began running from the room. Half beetles and creatures holding on to their patchy fur careened into one another, recoiling at every touch between fuzz and scaly carapace. None of them seemed interested in attacking or defending anyone now; they were all too intent on escape.

And then the huge room before us was empty and silent, only us humans and Alcibiades left behind. I had to look closely to make sure none of us had started exchanging traits—that none of us humans had suddenly grown fur or scales, and that Alcibiades hadn't grown a foot or a hand at the end of one of his slimy tentacles.

We hadn't. None of us looked any different than we had back on Earth or Zacadi, except for the total bafflement on everyone's faces.

"What was that all about?" Enu asked. He clutched my arm. "Did we just win or lose?"

"I don't think they were running off to get help for Zacadians or humans," Alcibiades said glumly. "So whatever happened to all of them, we lost."

His tentacles slumped. Even in prison I hadn't seen him looking so defeated.

"Nonsense," a voice said behind us. "Don't you understand that you just proved your point exactly?"

We all spun around. A mint-green Fred stood before us, completely covered in fur except for a small missing patch on one wrist—the kind of defect you might see on a stuffed animal that was carried around too much.

"You succeeded completely," the Fred told us briskly. "Which is not always the same thing as winning."

Rosi's eyes widened.

"Mrs. Osemwe?" she exclaimed.

And then she flung herself at the Fred-woman, wrapping her arms around the creature in a giant hug.

CHAPTER
FIFTY-TWO

Edwy tugged on Rosi's arm, trying to pull her back from the Fred.

"Rosi, *no*," he cried. "You've gone delirious. Or crazy. Or *something*. You think this is Mrs. Osemwe, the principal of our school back in Fredtown? She always looked *human*, remember? Because she was wearing a costume? And the Freds were lying to us all along, and . . ."

"Lying Freds?" Enu said, clenching his hands into fists again and peering hopefully in my direction.

I shook my head at him, but it was a reflex more than anything else.

"I. Don't. Understand," I said.

Rosi stayed in the Fred-woman's arms, but turned her face to peer back at the rest of us.

"Cana, Bobo, and I saw what Mrs. Osemwe really looked like when we were running away from Cursed Town," she said. "Remember, Cana?"

Cana peeked around toward the Fred-woman's back.

"That was just a hologram of Mrs. Osemwe," she said suspiciously. "Not real."

"This is the real me," the Fred-woman said. "I couldn't travel to Earth—er, well, I chose to believe I couldn't travel to Earth. I refused to even consider taking that risk. But I'm here now. I came to petition the court weeks ago, but I wasn't clever enough to figure out a way to get them to hear me."

Cana ran over and threw her arms around both Mrs. Osemwe and Rosi. The little girl tilted her head back, looking up at mint-green fur.

"Can you fix everything now?" Cana whispered.

"No," Mrs. Osemwe said. "Because the six of you already have. This is what's happening on Earth and Zacadi, this very moment."

She reached out and gently took my phone from my hand. She swiped a hand—or was it a paw?—across the screen, tapped in a few commands, then pointed the phone at the same blank wall I had used earlier.

"Earth's on the left," she said. "Zacadi is on the right."

She didn't need to tell us, because I recognized both scenes on the wall: the broad, open streets of Refuge City, the windswept wasteland of Zacadi. But the action on each side was similar: In each scene, Enforcers in dark uniforms ran toward what appeared to be some sort of space portal, which zapped them away. I didn't fully understand until I saw other Enforcers running onto spaceships as well. And then the spaceships took off.

On both planets, the Enforcers were running away. And they were so desperate to flee, they were using every method they could.

Enu stumbled over and touched the wall, as if that would help him understand.

"Is this real?" he asked. Now the scenes of retreating Enforcers flickered across his stunned face. "Is it true?"

"Yeah," Edwy agreed. "The intergalactic court accused Kiandra of faking her video—how do we know you're not faking this?"

Oh, my brothers, I thought. *You're so much alike.*

We Watanabonesets were all alike—I wanted to know the same thing.

But Alcibiades also flung his tentacles toward the wall and the Zacadi scene, as if he could shove the departing Enforcers away even faster. As if that would help him believe too.

Mrs. Osemwe raised the phone, temporarily aiming the scenes from our home planets onto the ceiling.

"Let me insert an additional app and energy boost into this phone, and I can prove this to you," she said. "You can contact anyone you're concerned about back on your home planets."

"Bobo," Rosi whispered, even as tears sprang to her eyes. "I can reach Bobo? Finally?"

"Our friend Udans," I added. And then I surprised myself by adding, "And my parents."

"Anyone who was imprisoned with me," Alcibiades said, his face stony. "Any Zacadian who's left at all."

Mrs. Osemwe nodded sadly.

"This will take a few moments," she said. "But I'll work as fast as I can."

She shut off the images glowing from my phone and laid it down on the podium.

"Can you answer questions while you work?" Rosi asked. "What changed? *How* did we make that happen?"

"Why are the Enforcers running away?" I asked. "Did the intergalactic court believe us after all?"

"What happened to the court, anyway?" Alcibiades asked. "Why were they so upset about how they looked?"

"And why did they change so much after we broke the window?" Cana asked.

Mrs. Osemwe glanced toward Edwy.

"Go ahead," she said wearily. "I'm sure you have about fifty questions too."

Edwy flashed her his saintliest smile.

"Believe it or not, I know how to take turns now," he said. "You can answer everyone else's questions first."

Mrs. Osemwe raised an eyebrow in surprise, then patted him on the back. Then he surprised me by hugging her as well.

"Where to start?" Mrs. Osemwe muttered, even as she returned to working on the phone. "I suppose you need to know the background. . . . We discovered recently that long before our first interactions with humans or Zacadians, all the peoples represented on the intergalactic court were descended from the same ancient species."

"Freds and Enforcers are the *same*?" Edwy exploded.

Mrs. Osemwe tilted her head to the side.

"Believe me, it was a surprise to us, too," she said wryly. "But the scholarship is impeccable. Unimpeachable. We *began* the same, but took vastly different paths as we spread across the galaxies."

"But—but—the way you and the Enforcers look . . . ," Enu stammered. "It's like comparing a *Tyrannosaurus rex* and, I don't know, baby chicks."

"Which human scientists discovered are *also* related to each other," Mrs. Osemwe said approvingly. "Young man, that is the perfect analogy. I can tell you must be a whiz at school."

Enu and I both stifled giggles. I'm pretty sure Mrs. Osemwe didn't see, because she bent low over the phone.

I'm also pretty sure Enu had had no clue that dinosaurs

and birds were related. But at least his confusion was wearing off, and he was making sense again.

"The difference," Mrs. Osemwe continued, "is that the Enforcers' and Freds' common ancestor had a trait that we've never found in unrelated species. There's nothing like it on Zacadi"—she dipped her head apologetically toward Alcibiades—"but you humans might see a resemblance to one type of Earth creature. The chameleon."

"Chameleons can change how they look," Cana said, as if she were reciting facts in school. "My teacher said some people think it's to hide from other animals that might eat them. And other people think it's to keep from getting too hot or cold, or to send a message to other chameleons. . . . Can *you* change the color of your fur any time you want, Mrs. Osemwe?"

"Not exactly," Mrs. Osemwe said, smiling gently at the little girl. "Chameleons can change back and forth pretty quickly. For Freds and Enforcers, what we look like reflects our entire life."

"Those court people changed instantly!" Edwy said, pointing out into the empty chambers, where we'd watched everyone morph from human appearance to a wide variety of fur and scales.

"Because you were seeing them change to their truest forms," Mrs. Osemwe said.

"Everything else we ever saw of them was a costume, right?" Rosi asked. "Or an illusion. Or what Edwy was telling us about, where microbes in the air distorted our view."

"Until we broke the window," Alcibiades bragged.

"Yes," Mrs. Osemwe said. She looked down at the bare, furless part of her arm. "When everything about how we live our lives is reflected in our appearance, we had to learn how to . . . hide sometimes, to have any privacy at all."

"So when we saw everyone there at the end, when they all screamed and panicked and ran away—that was almost like they thought we'd seen everyone naked, right?" Edwy asked.

I decided not to point out that he'd failed to wait for Mrs. Osemwe to answer everyone else's questions first.

"Yes, that would be the comparable human experience," Mrs. Osemwe said. "Except that it was even worse for the Freds and the Enforcers and the others here in the courtroom. It was like they were naked and every bad thing they'd ever done was written on their skin. In giant letters."

"I didn't see any writing," Enu said. Which probably gave Mrs. Osemwe a better idea of how Enu always did in school.

"You mean the fur or scales—those are just symbols?" Cana asked.

"Not *just* symbols, but yes, that's how it works," Mrs. Osemwe said. "When I was a child, my little brother was annoying me one day, and I pinched him. He was too little to talk yet, so he couldn't tell anyone. But one patch of my fur fell out, and my parents knew instantly that I'd done something wrong."

"If I'd been a Fred kid, I would have been totally furless by the time of my first birthday!" Edwy said.

"So that bare space on your arm—that's from something you did as a little kid?" I asked. "And that's the *only* bad thing you ever did?"

"No, no," Mrs. Osemwe laughed. "That was just my baby fur affected—like how you humans have baby teeth and adult teeth. We start over as adults. Freds practice as kids and then work very hard as adults to preserve their full fur. It's a point of pride. Just as the Enforcers pride themselves on being tough and . . . emotionless."

I thought about this system. It wouldn't be such a bad thing to know instantly, just by looking at someone, if they were kind or mean.

That's sort of how people in Cursed Town saw the world, believing that whether or not someone had green eyes determined whether they were good or bad, I realized. They wanted humans to be that simple.

But it didn't really work that way for humans. For humans, all of that was a lie. Even when humans tried out genetic alterations to get the "right" eye color, they'd just had more to fight about.

The system Mrs. Osemwe was talking about was real—how Freds and Enforcers looked really did reflect how they behaved.

"So the Enforcers are *proud* of being mean?" Rosi asked. Her voice shook, as if this idea frightened her.

"They are proud of being *strong*," Mrs. Osemwe corrected. "They interpret the symbols differently. They think fur is a sign of weakness. And stupidity. Naïveté. Which . . . maybe sometimes it was."

"But everyone worked together on the intergalactic court," I said, and for some reason my voice came out too loud, and every bit as shaky as Rosi's. "The Freds and the Enforcers—and all the other species that were like the Freds, and all the other species that were like the Enforcers—they all made decisions together. They agreed on things. To let the Freds take human children away, and then to send them back. To—"

"To let the Enforcers destroy my planet and steal the Zacadi pearls. And enslave my people and work them to death," Alcibiades interrupted. He slashed one tentacle through the air in a way that made me think of a judge pounding a gavel and pronouncing a guilty sentence.

Mrs. Osemwe dropped her head. Her hands stilled. I saw that she'd disassembled my phone, but hadn't started putting it back together again. It was in so many tiny pieces, I didn't see how it could ever work again.

"We were wrong," Mrs. Osemwe whispered. "We never understood humans or Zacadians. Both your species—you have such capacity for good, and such capacity for evil. Freds and Enforcers . . . we always believed you could only be one thing."

"The Enforcers are evil," Enu growled. "You actually thought the Freds were good?"

"We tried," Mrs. Osemwe said. She spread her arms like she wanted to hug us all. "We saw all the pain on Earth, and we thought we could help."

"You made my parents' pain worse," Rosi said. I'd never seen her speak so unflinchingly, so . . . unkindly. And yet it didn't seem as though she wanted to cause Mrs. Osemwe pain. She just wanted her to know the truth.

"And did you think that anything the Enforcers did on my planet would help the Zacadians?" Alcibiades asked incredulously.

"We trusted the Enforcers to report to us about everything on Zacadi," Mrs. Osemwe said. "We shouldn't have, but we thought if we looked too closely, it would . . . hurt us, too. It would make us lose our fur."

And suddenly I understood.

"But in the intergalactic court, the Freds and the Enforcers rubbed off on each other," I said. "Being around the Enforcers made the Freds make decisions that weren't entirely kind. And being around the Freds made some of the Enforcers a little nicer. None of you were purely one-sided anymore. Even the Enforcers who met us when our spaceship landed were nicer than the ones we ran away from on Zacadi."

"Yes," Mrs. Osemwe said. Meticulously she put together two pieces of my phone that seemed almost too small to matter. "Everyone in the intergalactic court complex changed in some way. And in the Fredtowns we built for the human children, we found that *they* rubbed off on us too, and even though we thought we were being entirely kind and generous in raising them, they changed us too, in ways we didn't expect." She touched the bare patch on her arm. "This wasn't because of anything I did wrong, necessarily. It was because I came to understand humans. And . . . discovered that some of my most badly behaved students could also be among my favorites."

Edwy grinned as though she'd complimented him personally.

Oh—maybe she had. Yeah, that seemed about right: Edwy was probably the *worst*-behaved kid in his Fredtown school.

"But why would any of that make the Enforcers leave Earth?" Enu asked. "Or Zacadi?"

"Because we Freds and the other species like us were

always more powerful than the Enforcers and their ilk," Mrs. Osemwe said. "Living in peace gives a culture more space and freedom to develop its technology. We had the power, but we told ourselves it was nobler not to use it. You children forced us to see ourselves and our actions as they really are. And once you've seen the truth, you can no longer live a lie."

Cana squinted up at Mrs. Osemwe.

"Was that a principle of Fredtown?" she asked.

"No," Mrs. Osemwe said. "But it should have been."

"Oh," Cana said. "I'll remember it, then."

Mrs. Osemwe patted Cana's head. Then she held up my phone, miraculously reassembled.

"Who wants to make the first call?" she asked.

EPILOGUE—ONE YEAR LATER

I kicked off my dusty boots and dived for the most comfortable chair in the living room.

"Dibs!" I yelled, just in case Enu or Edwy had any bright ideas about beating me to it.

"No fair," Edwy groaned behind me. He put down his bucket with a heavy thud and began pulling off his own boots. "Enu and I worked twice as long as you!"

"You worked *outside* for twice as long as me," I corrected, snuggling into the cozy chair. "It's not my fault you haven't learned to work on electronics equipment indoors yet."

"I can't believe we saved two planets from Enforcers, and I'm *still* picking up Zacadi pearls every day!" Enu grumbled.

But his words held no bite. It was a joking complaint, just as Edwy's and my taunts were more for fun than anything else.

"Oh, stuff it," I said. "You're getting bigger muscles than ever, and you know we see you admiring yourself in the mirror every morning."

"And you can ask to transfer to a different job any time you want," Edwy added. "That's the difference."

We were back on Zacadi once again, but *everything* was different now. Our jobs were only part-time, after school—not full-time enslavement.

And we had chosen this.

After the Enforcers fled from Zacadi, a humanitarian group of Freds landed to help the small group of surviving Zacadians, as well as the remaining human prisoners. All the humans wanted to return to Earth, and the Freds sent them back right away. But the sick, starving Zacadians were in such desperate straits that they couldn't run their planet on their own, so they agreed to an experiment: People from all over the universe would try to build a new civilization here, one where various intelligent species worked together.

I was the first volunteer.

"You can't bear to be separated from your buddy Alcibiades, huh?" Enu had teased me, but I didn't even bother responding, because he was busy signing up second.

Edwy signed up third.

None of us actually said it out loud, but I think we all knew: We couldn't have gone back to the safe blandness of our lives in Refuge City after everything we'd gone through. We were Watanabonesets: We needed challenges.

The amazing thing was that, once they found out they

could finally escape Cursed Town, our parents followed us to Zacadi as well.

Our mother stepped in the back door from the garden just then, holding a bucket full of tomatoes.

"Don't get too comfortable," she said. "I still need help picking green beans."

We all groaned. We were all still getting used to having parents around, in our faces all the time.

The Freds who were in charge of helping everyone make a smooth transition assured us that what we were feeling was normal and natural for human teenagers—a category that even Edwy fit into now.

Just when I thought I couldn't bear dealing with my parents for one more instant, they would look at us the way my mother was looking at us now: her face soft, her eyes glowing.

Our parents loved us. They always had. They'd sacrificed for us, even when they'd believed they'd never see us again.

I stood up and headed for the garden, a tangle of vines and greenery. It *was* a miracle how my mother had managed to coax life out of the dead Zacadi soil. She had done so well that she gave classes now in the town hall, helping other new citizens learn to grow their own food. In all our video chats over the years, she'd always seemed like such the lady of leisure, so it amused me to see her now with a constant rim of dirt under her fingernails.

But that wasn't nearly as funny as what my father was doing now: The Freds had made him police chief of our new town.

Even he had protested that one: "But, but . . . don't you know what I did back on Earth?"

"Yes," the Fred who was handling job assignments told him. "We know you understand how the criminal mind works. You will be great at this."

And . . . he was. So far the only crimes in our community had been on the level of little kids stealing apples from their neighbors' trees, but my dad had solved those in nothing flat.

It was a big switch to have a father I could be proud of.

Out in the garden I grabbed a bag and began snapping beans off the vine. A head bobbed over the fence to the yard next door, disappeared, then came into view again.

"Hi—"

"Ki—"

"—an—"

"—dra!"

It was Rosi's little brother, Bobo, jumping up and down and calling out to me every time he spied me over the fence. He did this a lot—he liked proving that he could handle the extra Zacadian gravity. And proving that we were friends.

A second later Rosi herself appeared in the neighboring backyard. She lifted Bobo in her arms.

"Sorry," she said. "Is he bothering you?"

"I'm always happy to see Bobo," I said, grinning at the little boy. I could have added a *now, anyway,* but none of that mattered anymore.

Bobo was the first person we'd tried to track down that day we were at the intergalactic court and Mrs. Osemwe had managed to convert my phone into a communication device capable of reaching other planets. We'd spent a tense and stressful hour calling people all over Refuge City, hearing accounts of children in jails, children beaten and barely alive. But Zeba had been the exact right person to leave Bobo with, because she and her parents knew a whole network of people who lived under the radar, outside the view of any authority.

Bobo had been sitting in a soup kitchen eating blueberry pie when we'd finally found him. He was fine.

But I saw the way Rosi still held him a little too tightly, even now. And I saw the way Bobo squeezed her shoulders. But then he began to squirm.

"Rosi!" he complained. "I want to run and bounce some more!"

"Of course you do," Rosi said, giving him one last hug and then letting him jump to the ground.

"You could be with him all the time this summer if you start that teacher-training internship," I told Rosi across the fence.

"I know," Rosi said. She rolled her eyes, which reminded me that, like Edwy, she was a teenager now too. "I love Bobo and all the other kids—but that's not what I want to do the rest of my life."

"It isn't?" I asked. "But you're so good with little kids!"

"I kind of had to be, back in Fredtown, because Edwy and I were the oldest," she said. "But I like other things too. . . . Did I tell you Alcibiades volunteered to teach me how spaceships work this summer?"

"Really? That's great!" I exclaimed. An idea began forming in my mind. "So, say, ten years from now, when this place is all settled and boring, you and Alcibiades and I—and whoever else wants to go—we'll be explorers across the universe, finding all sorts of new civilizations. You two fly the ship; I'll be the communications officer. . . ."

"Sounds good to me," Rosi said. "If we wait until Cana grows up too, she can be our translator."

"I'll be the security officer," Enu said behind me.

"And I'll be the spy," Edwy said, sneaking out of the house alongside him. "Admit it—you're going to need a spy."

Rosi and I just laughed. But it wasn't a bad plan.

"More picking, less talking," Mom jokingly called out the kitchen window. "We're having company for dinner tonight."

"Zeba's family?" I asked.

"And Udans," Mom said.

To our great joy, we'd found out that he had survived the Enforcer invasion of Refuge City as well, and my parents had begged him to join us on Zacadi. They didn't treat him as an employee anymore, though—he was more like a favorite uncle now.

I guess the fact that he'd saved Enu's, Edwy's, and my life had changed everything.

Or maybe my parents had always cared about him—as much as they could, back on Earth, especially in Cursed Town. Maybe it was being on Zacadi that had changed everything.

It had changed how I saw Udans, anyway.

Enu, Edwy, and I were just handing over bulging containers of green beans to Mom when our doorbell rang.

"It's Alcibiades," Edwy said, glancing toward the front window.

"Oooh, Kiandra, I bet he's here for you," Enu teased.

I slugged him in the arm and opened the door.

"Do you want to go greet the newest arrivals?" he asked. "They're landing in fifteen minutes."

"Sure," I said. I knew a lot of words in his language now, but as I headed out the door, I still switched on the automatic translator I wore around my neck. It prevented any misunderstandings from getting out of hand. It was kind of like how we could breathe the Zacadi air without much difficulty, but we still kept emergency packs around that mimicked Earth's atmosphere, just in case any of us started having problems.

"Did you hear the council finally voted on our town's name today?" Alcibiades asked.

"That took long enough!" I groaned. "How many meetings have they had about that? And let me guess—they still probably went with New Zacadi City."

"No," Alcibiades said softly. "They went with the human name."

"You mean Jubilee?" I said, surprised. I tried it out. "So now we live in Jubilee City. . . . Are you sure you don't mind? I mean, this *is* still your planet, and so much of your civilization is gone. . . ."

"No, it's perfect," Alcibiades said. "All my people agreed."

After the last attack by the Enforcers, only sixty Zacadians remained. But the Fred-healers assured them there was no reason those sixty wouldn't live to ripe old ages and someday have children of their own. The Zacadians were not going to go extinct.

"You like the name Jubilee City because . . . you want to celebrate surviving at all?" I asked.

"That, and we liked the other meaning your word can have," Alcibiades said. His eyes slid up and down in a way that I'd learned to recognize as signaling happiness. "We liked the part about being freed from the mistakes of the past, and starting new."

"This *is* new," I said, looking around at all the half-built houses started on the new streets radiating out from ours.

I raised my hand to wave at Rosi and Bobo's parents, sitting on the porch of the house next door. Then I remembered that Rosi's father was blind, and I called out, "Hello, Mr. and Mrs. Alvaran."

It *was* amazing that Rosi's parents, who had been so injured in the war in their hometown all those years ago, could live side by side with my parents, who had become wealthy from the war. I wouldn't say they were exactly best friends, but I had heard Rosi's mother and mine call out greetings across the fence.

It was a start.

"Oh, and they announced the teachers for the new school year," Alcibiades said. "Cana's mom was on the list for helping out in the teenagers' classroom."

Cana's mom had been a maid back on Earth, but everyone was discovering new skills on Zacadi.

"Good," I said. "She's smart like Cana. I bet she'll know how to make it fun."

Alcibiades and I reached the town square and joined a crowd gathering on the beginnings of a lawn. The spaceship had already landed, and the landing ramp was lowered. The first person stepped into the doorway, and Alcibiades and I gasped at the same time.

"What? Enforcers? They're allowing Enforcers to come now?" Alcibiades asked. "Why would they do that?"

The creature had a face like a beetle, but as he walked down the ramp, I saw that the rest of his body was divided between fur and scales.

"*Is* he actually still an Enforcer, if he's changed that much?" I asked under my breath.

The creature stumbled toward the crowd. For some reason, his gaze honed in on Alcibiades and me. He stopped right in front of us, while the rest of the crowd watched silently. He held up the translator hanging around his neck.

"I am a teenager," he said, the words spilling out of the translator. "Is that what you are too?"

I thought about how much I'd feared and hated the Enforcers back on Earth and during my time as a prisoner on Zacadi. I thought about how much of my parents' lives had been spent hating all the same people they'd hated during their war.

And then I thought about how this boy was too young to have committed any of the Enforcer crimes on Earth or Zacadi. He wasn't to blame for anything his people had done, any more than I was to blame for anything my parents had done back on Earth.

"Yes, we're like you, and you're like us," I told him. I forced the corners of my mouth up into a smile, and it felt genuine. It *was* genuine. "Welcome to Jubilee."

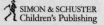

CAN AN UNDERCOVER NERD BECOME A SUPERSTAR AGENT? FIND OUT IN STUART GIBBS'S *NEW YORK TIMES* BESTSELLING SPY SCHOOL SERIES!